THE OTHER SIDE OF HER

One Secret, Two Twisted Stories, and
A Dangerous Obsession

ASHNA PREM

BLUEROSE PUBLISHERS
India | U.K.

Copyright © Ashna Prem 2025

All rights reserved by author. No part of this publication may be reproduced, stored in a retrieval system or transmitted in any form or by any means, electronic, mechanical, photocopying, recording or otherwise, without the prior permission of the author. Although every precaution has been taken to verify the accuracy of the information contained herein, the publisher assumes no responsibility for any errors or omissions. No liability is assumed for damages that may result from the use of information contained within.

BlueRose Publishers takes no responsibility for any damages, losses, or liabilities that may arise from the use or misuse of the information, products, or services provided in this publication.

For permissions requests or inquiries regarding this publication, please contact:

BLUEROSE PUBLISHERS
www.BlueRoseONE.com
info@bluerosepublishers.com
+91 8882 898 898
+4407342408967

ISBN: 978-93-6783-685-9

Cover design: Shubham
Typesetting: Sagar

First Edition: January 2025

To my Ninni
My bff, my sister, my mentor
Thank you for encouraging me to think crazy
And for always being by my side

Acknowledgment

First and foremost, I want to express my deepest gratitude to Amma, Acha and my brother Vinay. Your unwavering support since my day one and endless patience has been the backbone of this journey. I am extremely grateful to have you guys as my strongest pillars.

To my dear friends Devika, Anusha, Dula and Ronak, thank you for believing in me even when I doubted myself. Thank you Rithika for recommending 'The Silent Patient' to me, as I would not have explored more thrillers if it wasn't for that. You guys offered me words of encouragement when I needed them most, especially during those times when I was afraid to move forward and doubted myself. Your love and encouragement mean the world to me.

To my publisher Blue Rose Publication, your guidance, expertise, and sharp eye have truly brought this book to life. Your dedication and hard work behind the scenes have made this book possible.

Lastly, to my readers, Thank You for choosing to spend your time with Ahaana, Vihaan and Annie. Your curiosity and enthusiasm are the reason this story exists. I hope it resonates with you as much as it has with me.

Chapter - 1

Ahaana

It was a small one line text message flashing on her brand new iPhone with the slightest 'ting' sound. One look at the name of the sender and Ahaana paused in the middle of stirring her tea. Suddenly her favorite ceramic pastel pink mug felt too heavy in her hand, she could feel her heart beat unnaturally fast against her chest on this boring Tuesday afternoon. Could it be true? Ahaana was never one to not trust herself or her senses but right now she doubted if her eyes were messing with her, deceiving her because only she knew how long she waited to see that name flash on her phone screen in the form of a call or a message. And after all these years here it is.

She placed the mug of steaming hot tea on the polished mahogany table at her now almost one-year old new office in Bangalore and slowly picked up her phone, processing how monumental this moment was. She pulled the phone closer to see if she really read the name right. It was right there. 'Message from Vihaan'. Ahaana's vision instantly became blurry and she realized that her mouth was shaking and so were her fingers and her eyes were starting to tear up. There was a concoction of emotions brewing inside her. A little bit of warmth, the satisfaction of knowing he is alive and reaching out to her for something, a little bit of sadness and hurt when the memories came flooding back to her of that miserable day, remembering the things that were said to one another and the actions that followed, but above all her tiny little heart was bursting with so much happiness.

She opened the message and it was very short, concise and crisp but it told her more than she needed to know. A really short message that simply said "Didi, I need you. Please…" Her little brother needed her help. What could have possibly happened that he came to her now? Was he hurt? Was he even safe? But most importantly he is asking her out of all the people which could only mean that something had happened that was beyond him and he trusted that his sister was the only one who could fix it for him. Meaning it was personal this time. And of course, she would fix it, if it's for her dear Vihaan, nothing was impossible for her.

Ahaana called him because she did not wish to spend another moment typing up a reply when she could hear his voice this instant. She wondered what his voice might sound like now. Last time she heard him talk he was barely 20, still transitioning into an adult and so was his voice. Coarse and childlike at the same time. Ahaana wondered if she would even recognize him if she were to meet him now, would he have become taller now? He was always the tall one in the house. 10 years have gone by without a single call and a message from Vihaan. She had been vigorously working hard to prove a point to her family and she thought that once she made enough money to settle down well with her own house and her own reputation, that she would finally be able to leave everything behind. Little did she know back then that no amount of money or fame can buy her the love and appreciation of her family and that life would start feeling very empty indeed without her favorite people in it.

He must've picked up on the fourth or fifth ring because Ahaana was suddenly pulled back into reality when she heard a man's voice on the other end of the line. 'Hello... Didi?' Ahaana had to almost pinch her hand to remind herself to reply and in a croaking voice she asked 'Vihaan, where are you? What happened? Are you OK?' Vihaan could hear his sister's voice full of love and concern that he never really received from their own mother and he realized immediately how badly he wanted to give his big sister a tight hug. He was practically crying when he replied 'Didi... I miss you... I want..to see...you... I'm sorry Didi. Sorry for everything I did to you' Ahaana is a pretty solid woman and being in the kind of profession that she is in, nothing can easily shake her up except when she heard her brother break down. There was no more holding back now. 10 years' worth of worry and anxiety instantly melted into tears. And just like that she felt like they were back in their parent's house, a 3 year old Vihaan and an 8 year old Ahaana, in their room feeling scared while thunder was striking outside on a dark rainy night when their parents were arguing loudly in the next room and little Vihaan came running and crying into his sister's arms. She would hug him tightly and say "Hey. Its Alright! I am here for you. I won't let anything bad happen to you. I promise !"

Chapter - 2

Annie

Annie's head was pulsing hard. It was always the same with Alex. Every time he called and started with the saint-who-is-only-trying-to-save-her bullshit she would feel her patience ebbing away and the nerves at her temples tightening giving way to a nagging headache that will stay with her like a shadow for the whole day. Getting separated from Alex was not a walk in the park for Annie too but she hated it when he played the victim card in front of people. Annie always knew that she had issues with control and temper but who doesn't? Moving to Mumbai was Alex's idea. 'Big city means big opportunities', 'Don't you want us to start living our dream life?', 'Once you move to Mumbai it will be so good that you'll never want to come back to this life again. I promise.' What she didn't know while she mindlessly nodded along to these honey coated promises was that she was heading towards a darkness that would only engulf her the more she tried to run away from it.

On November 2014, Annie and Alex moved to Mumbai from Jaipur for Alex's new job. Annie was a housewife. She had never worked before in her life. She loved dancing and always dreamed of owning her own studio someday. 'In this country us middle class people don't get to dream this big, beta. Your priority right now should be to get married into a good house with a good family. And if you're lucky your husband might even support your dreams.' Her mother used to tell her. Brainwashed, Annie did the same thing which every small town girl with big dreams ultimately ends up doing. Married the guy that was chosen for her by her parents and followed her husband to the new city which promised them everything. Which promised her everything she ever wanted.

But Annie realized soon enough that things were a little off from the beginning itself. Alex had promised her a really nice apartment in one of the nicest parts of the city, close to his office where he would help her get started on her dance studio. But Annie found herself walking into a dusty, old, extremely cramped 1 BHK apartment in the shabbier side of the city which was almost an hour's drive in Mumbai's swarming traffic from Alex's office. She did not like the cramped spaces or the neighborhood but what choice did she have? She would confront Alex about the apartment situation, 'Its just temporary Annie, the broker was a fraud and now I cannot get hold of him. But don't you worry, I will figure something out soon' Alex would say. Their days in that tight old apartment felt nothing like the sweet promises that he had made to her before leaving their home in Jaipur. It was almost like a dark curtain had fallen over her dreams of starting fresh and bright in a young city. Coming from a small town in Jaipur and having had to constantly fight a hundred times for anything that she wanted in life, Annie was never one to give up that easily. Had it been just the apartment or the neighborhood, Annie would have still held on to the silver lining but little did she know about the surprises that were lurking behind the mirage of this 'new beginning'.

Annie took a deep breath and pulled herself back to the present realizing that she was digging her nails deep into her hand in tightly clenched fists. She opened her eyes and replied to Alex who was still patiently waiting on the call to hear her decision. 'Fine! Yes I will go see the psychiatrist like you want me to. Is that all?' Alex sighed and tried to sound normal but the pain in his voice was very much evident, 'Annie, I know that you think I'm this monster for some reason and you hate me. Believe it or not I regret that night very deeply for letting you go and I am extremely sorry for hurting you but I still care about you even though we're not together anymore. We don't need to be stuck in the past and I really want you to go forward in life and get everything that you always wished for. But before that you need this help. I cannot disown you like your family did and I never wanted this divorce in the first place. I still don't want it. You know that I only agreed to this for you. Because you were stubborn about it. Annie maybe this doctor can make you understand things better.' Annie couldn't believe what she was hearing. Is this asshole for real? Who is he trying to fool here? As if her head wasn't already throbbing in pain she felt a fresh dose of pain shoot up at her temples. She needed to get rid of this guy from her life as quickly as she could and if that meant she had to go see a doctor like she was some lunatic as he was trying to make her look, then fine, she'll do it.

The only thing that kept her going was the alimony she would receive which could really help her start fresh again and live a new life somewhere. That, and Daisy's sweet innocent angelic face. Annie knew on some level that getting custody of Daisy was a long shot. She did not have anything to prove herself innocent after what happened that horrible night. It was a spur of the moment thing and almost an accident. But Annie was her mother after all and what law would keep a mother away from her daughter? She hated the idea of Daisy living with Alex and whoever would walk into his life next after her. Her mind would never be at peace knowing that Daisy is still with her father. It was a long shot but if seeing this psychiatrist is going to help her prove that she is not insane after all then she'll do it so that she can fight for the custody of her darling daughter.

'Alex, I told you that I will go see the doctor, right? So please stop nagging me about this. I have to go now.' She hung up the call and the room fell right back into the silence it was in a little while ago, only difference being, there was a lot of tension in this silence now. Annie closed her eyes and rubbed her temples. Took a few deep breaths. Nothing. The pain wasn't going away anytime soon. But she didn't have the liberty to sit around at home like before. She needed to get to work now. She swallowed her painkiller in one swift gulp of water and walked out of the apartment.

Chapter - 3

Vihaan

Vihaan felt a wave of relief wash over him after that phone call with his sister. He had no idea how that call would go. Would she even spare a minute to talk to her brother who was too quick to disown her 10 years ago? But somewhere Vihaan always knew that no matter what happened to him, if there was one person on this planet who would rush to save him in a heartbeat, that would be his sister. And now he feels deeply embarrassed for losing out on all these years with her, for pretending that he did not even have a sister for 10 long years.

But all is well that ends well right? Sure, he created a lot of distress for Ahaana, he literally made life hell for her, but now is his chance to make things right and even bring her home after all this time. The last part might take a little bit more convincing, knowing how stubborn and proud his sister can be. He smiled a little at the thought of that. But he also realized that he was starting to feel very hopeful at the thought of meeting her soon.

Vihaan was looking out the big French windows opening into the lush green lawn lined with pine trees. The world just seemed a lot more colorful today, all of a sudden. It was looking like a happy picture made by a happy child. Blue sky with fluffy cotton clouds, he could hear the humming of a bird close by. Was this new or were there always birds around this place, he wondered? The golden light was flooding in through the French windows and Vihaan just sat there soaking in the whole scene unfurling in front of him. He was the most relaxed in months today and he really wished Helen was also there to share this moment with him. Helen! Oh my god !! He totally forgot to call her. He reached out to get his phone and there were 5 missed calls and 23 messages from Helen. He didn't even bother to check the messages and speed dialed Helen immediately.

'Hey! Are you okay? How did it go with your sister? Was she willing to talk to you? What did she say? Why didn't you call me?' Vihaan couldn't help but smile at how concerned she was for him. After all what did he do to deserve such an amazing woman in his life? 'Hey beautiful! Please calm down and breathe for a second. First of all, I'm so sorry that I didn't call you sooner. I am still processing that I just talked to my sister after 10 years. But yes, I think the call went great. We will meet up soon and I can tell her about everything then.' Helen was happy to know that Vihaan was happy. 'Babe, I'm so glad that you convinced me to do this. If it wasn't for you, I don't think I would've had the courage to reach out to her.' There was a lot of gratitude in Vihaan's voice.

'Of course, babe. I mean, she is your sister after all. And this has been going on for way too long. Enough already.'

'Yes, you're right. You always are' Vihaan had a playful smile as he said this.

'So, what are you up to now?' asked Helen quickly picking up on his good mood.

'Well, I'm just chilling here enjoying the sun wishing you were here to make me your famous coffee that I love so much.'

'Oh, so it's just the coffee that you're missing and not me? Huh?' said Helen in a slight mock irritation.

Vihaan always loved pulling her leg and getting her pissed off at him for no reason at all. He burst out laughing and said 'I'm kidding babe. I miss you! Come home soon. Let's have coffee and go out for dinner tonight.'

'Are you asking me out on a date on a Tuesday Mr. Workaholic?' teased Helen.

'Hey hey, I'm not a workaholic, I'm just very focused and take my work seriously when I'm doing it. That's all. Work hard and play harder right?'

Now it was Helen's turn to blush, 'Okay that's enough playboy. I'll be there in 10. Where are we making reservations?'

'I'm craving a lot of sushi after hearing Sid rave about this new Japanese place that opened up. You, me, sushi, what do you say?'

'Uh…Sushi and me Vihaan? Um…okay…. I guess they might have other stuff on their menu, too right?'

'Why?' asked a perplexed Vihaan.

Helen was quiet to give him a moment to figure it out.

'Oh my god! I'm so sorry!! I totally forgot about your allergy for a second there. Okay Sushi is cancelled. Let's hit our favorite spot then. What do you say?'

'You talked to your sister once and already forgot everything you knew about me?' teased Helen.

'Haha! You are not the kind of woman to be forgotten. You are the kind of woman to be cherished for as long as I live. Now come over soon please? I miss you already.'

'Okay Romeo!! Please save some for dessert too. I'll be there in a heartbeat.'

Chapter - 4

Ahaana
16 Years Ago

The first day of medical school was scary enough as it is for Ahaana Khanna. She always hated the idea of an academic year beginning during the onset of rains. If the beginning is bright, positive and sunny naturally the rest of the year should also follow suit according to her. But just like any other day in monsoon, it was heavily raining like it was the end of the world. By the time she reached her college in her black Mercedes, which was insisted by her father since he wanted to personally drop her off on her first day at college not just as a father to a future doctor but also as a proud alumnus, Ahaana regretted wearing the pure white Kurti because everywhere she looked she only saw pools of water and a lot of puddles. Ahaana was what one might call an effortless beauty. She had a short, slender frame but she had light skin with a naturally blushed cheeks and soft pink lips to compliment. She had long thick luscious hair and big piercing hazel brown eyes that could reach into your soul. She was not one to wear a lot of makeup because one, she did not care about it, and two, she wanted to be validated for her work instead of her looks because people always made her aware from a young age that she was very attractive. Today was a big day and Ahaana told herself to take a deep breath, reminded her nerves to calm down as she is here to study and not for a fashion show and nobody is going pay too much attention to her even though she is the daughter of the renowned Dr. Rajiv Khanna, only the best Psychiatrist in all of South Bombay, a title awarded to him by the IMA.

The rain had already made the Mumbai traffic worse than usual and Ahaana couldn't keep calm or cool inside the perfectly air-conditioned Mercedes. By the time she reached her school, she immediately knew that as a fresher she had failed to abide by the one primary rule that she was supposed to follow. Be on time! She said a quick goodbye to her father, who was still somewhere lost in his trip to memory lane, and ran towards the main block of the campus unaware of the fact that she had forgotten her umbrella.

Ahaana was finally inside the building and checked at the help desk to figure out where the orientation was happening. The lady at the desk gave Ahaana a disapproving look as if to say 'Seriously? That's how you're going to your first class?' Ahaana took a step back and looked at herself and instantly knew what the problem was. She was drenched and wet and white being an easily translucent color, betrayed her and gave her away, revealing her bra inside the kurti. She wished she had a dupatta or the doctor's coat but she had neither. So, she did what any girl with basic common sense would do and opened her long-wet hair to cover up what her kurti couldn't. Looking like a drenched dog wasn't the most fashionable way to start her academic year, but it was the best she could manage at the moment.

The lady told her that she'll need to go to the building across the open garden which is where the classes were happening. Already 20 mins late to her first class, Ahaana could not afford to wait until the rain ceased. She darted towards the building across the garden and in the rush, she lost her footing on the slippery ground. She slipped and fell on the muddy pavement with her bottom and her left elbow hitting hard on the ground. For a while she couldn't process what had happened and once she realized that she had fallen down and tried to get up, she felt a surge of excruciating pain in her right ankle. She accidentally let out a little scream when the pain shot up her leg. Her first day jitters along with this humiliating yet painful incident really broke down young Ahaana and feeling helpless she found herself crying in the rain on the muddy, stone pavement.

All of a sudden, she felt 2 strong arms swooping her up in one swift movement and was effortlessly lifted from the muddy pavement. She remembered not seeing another human being in the vicinity since everybody were in class already. How did this guy appear from thin air? She looked up and saw the most mesmerizing green eyes she had ever seen. He was easily 6 ft tall, clearly muscular and well built which was evident from the way he was carrying her and walking towards the nearest building like it was a piece of cake. He was wearing a black shirt and she could feel his biceps trying to tear up the sleeve as if trying to get out and catch some air. His face had a brooding but a strange aura to it. Like the kind of guy who was a little intimidating and you took him seriously but also like this beautiful specimen of a human being, the kind from which you just cannot avert your eyes even if you wanted to. Ahaana could tell he had a razor sharp jawline hidden behind that neatly trimmed and shaped beard and sculpted cheekbones and thick black hair that was trimmed sharply and with so much precision. This guy should have been a model what is he even doing here, thought Ahaana.

He walked towards the nearby student union block with Ahaana still in his arms, both of them soaking wet from the rain. He slowly but carefully lowered her on to a chair.

'Hey, are you OK? Asked the stranger with beautiful green eyes.

'Hi... ahem... yes I think I'm okay but it's my ankle...' Ahaana Khanna stammering and that too in front a guy? What effect is this guy having on her. Pull yourself together Ahaana, she scolded herself.

The mystery man had a very concerned look on his face as he listened to Ahaana. He took a quick look at her right leg and asked her, 'May I?' seeking permission to hold her ankle for a closer inspection.

Ahaana was still in a haze and nodded along. The man pulled the sleeve of his shirt up to his elbows revealing the most beautiful hands she had ever seen and gently took her leg in his hands. They looked like a fragile little dove inside his massive strong hands. He started mildly turning her ankle this way and that and on the second turn Ahaana let out a cry out of pain. But for some reason, he didn't look too worried now in fact there was even a slight hint of a smile playing on his lips. He looked at her and said, 'Well, your ankle seems to have twisted just a little during the fall which is why you are not able to turn it the other way. However, the good news is there are no signs of fracture.' Ahaana was puzzled. She wasn't able to think straight, distracted by this handsome stranger kneeling down in front of her with her leg in his hands. This is so not how she had planned her first day at medical school. Ahaana snapped back when she heard a muffled sound from him. She asked, 'I'm sorry I didn't hear you?'. He chuckled slightly and asked her in a very confident yet assuring voice, 'I said, do you trust me?' Ahaana didn't know what to say. He was after all a stranger. He could be a student there or a doctor but he did not look like one. Not with that body and face. He was probably a few years older than her. There was absolutely no one around to take her to the nurse's room and she was definitely not in a position to do it herself. If she had to carry on with her day she had to decide about her leg now. Being a control freak, trusting somebody was not Ahaana's best qualities. But certain circumstances force you to go out of your way sometimes. She took a deep breath, looked at him and said 'Yes!'. 'Good.' He said, 'Now this might hurt only like an ant bite, just take a deep breath and hold on to me alright? Just keep your eyes on me and do not look anywhere else.' He finished that sentence and twisted her ankle in the blink of an eye. And he was right. There was fresh doze of pain that shot up Ahaana's leg and she squeezed his bicep hard and closed her eyes shut and let out a small scream because it certainly felt nothing like an ant bite like he said, it was a lot more. Eyes still closed, Ahaana heard his smooth voice, but closer this time, he was closer to her ears now. 'Hey, its over. You're good as new'. Ahaana opened her eyes and looked at the stranger his face only inches away from hers and she thought she saw something change in his eyes, like he was admiring an exotic creature or witnessing something beautiful for the first time. Ahaana had to break off her gaze from him and she looked at her ankle, it looked normal at first but she was still scared to get up. 'Don't worry, it won't hurt now, please try getting up' and she did and he was right. There was absolutely no sign of pain. Ahaana was relieved. 'Thank you' smiling for the first time that morning Ahaana turned to look at him. 'No problem.' Smiled back the stranger.

But now she had to know who he was so she introduced herself to him,

'Hi! I'm Ahaana, first year student and as you probably guessed by now it is my first day here.'

'Hi! I'm Zayyan Khan, Final year student here' Zayyan extended his hand and Ahaana took it and they had the official introduction to each other.

Ahaana had completely lost track of time and it was not until her phone vibrated that she realized that she had missed the first hour of orientation. 'I think I should get to my orientation now, I'm really sorry that I'm running off like this.'

'Haha no problem Ahaana. I'll see you around I guess?'

'Yeah' said Ahaana with a twinkle in her eyes.

As she turned and started walking away in the opposite direction she heard Zayyan calling out her name, 'Ahaana wait a second'. She turned back to look at him and saw him rushing towards his bag nearby and picking up his neatly folded white coat and running towards her.

'It's your dress, I mean .. it's gotten a little dirty at the back with the mud and everything from when you fell down and you don't want to walk into your first class with that.'

It was at that moment Ahaana realized that she was as red as a tomato. She had totally forgotten about her translucent white kurti, and probably how dirty she must look now with literally splashes of mud all over her. And she was with Zayyan all this time completely unaware of how she looked in front of him. She wished at that moment that the earth would split in half and she could just disappear forever. As if catching up with Ahaana's thoughts by reading her shocked expression Zayyan laughed and wrapped his white coat around her. 'There you go. Problem solved. Now don't be late for your next class.' Zayyan smiled and gave her a little wink as he turned and started walking in the other direction.

Ahaana's head was spinning with too many emotions. She felt embarrassed but at the same time she also felt a burst of happiness inside her. Her heart was beating faster than ever. She felt new and she felt seen.

As she walked towards her class she pulled his coat closer around her and instantly got a whiff of his perfume. So that's what Zayyan smells like, and in a strange way she liked the fact that now she too smells like him too. Little did she know at that moment that her destiny had taken a turn.

Chapter - 5

Annie

It was a cold rainy morning in Mumbai. Annie had just woken up to her alarm, which was always set at a low volume so as to not wake up her friend and flat mate who was extremely kind enough to let her stay with her until she was able to find a place of her own. Days had turned into weeks and weeks had turned into months now, 3 months to be precise. Annie made herself a cup of tea like she usually does and had walked to the balcony like she always did but she soon realized that the rain had wet the floor of the balcony and she will have to stay indoors for now. That was one of the few things Annie loved about this apartment. It was a stark contrast to the tiny, dusty, mold filled apartment that she had moved into when she first moved to Mumbai 3 years ago with her husband. This place was clean, spacious and had a splendid view since it was on the twelfth floor. Usually as creatures of habitat, human beings will take time to settle in to a new place but not Annie, she felt more relaxed and easier in this new atmosphere almost to the extent where she did not wish to leave, but it was also not fair of her to overstay her friend's welcome. Mrs. Rodriguez who owned this beautiful and pristine apartment was a reserved lady in her early 80s, whom Annie used to meet at church. Mrs. Rodriguez was not much of a socializer but something about young and naïve Annie invited her in. She reminded her of her late daughter Josephine who passed away at an even younger age in a car accident. Josephine would've been Annie's age now, had she still been with her. Mr. Rodrigues had suffered a stroke soon after his daughter passed away and he too left poor Mrs. Rodriguez to live out her twilight years alone in this big city.

Annie watched at the waves of steam rising up from the hot cup enwrapped by her slender fingers. She took a long deep breath thinking over what lay ahead for her today. Alex had convinced her to go see the psychiatric doctor who was a friend of a friend. Apparently, that was supposed to make Annie feel more secure. It was probably the strangest 'informal' clause anyone would put in a divorce agreement. Alex claims that he still loves her and would love to take care of her but for Annie, that trust died a long time ago along with …. Nope! Not now. She shouldn't let her mind wander off to that night. Because that's when her headaches begin. 'Think of something else, anything but this', Annie muttered under her own breath.

'Good Morning dear! You are up early today!' said a voice from behind her oozing with warmth and motherly affection. Annie turned around to see Mrs. Rodriguez standing behind her still in her nightgown.

'Good Morning Aunty!' Annie said, relieved to have been yanked back to the present by a pleasant face.'

'Why do you look so worried? What happened dear?'

'Oh! Its nothing Aunty'

'No. I know when your face changes. Talk to me child.'

'Today is the day I have to go meet the doctor that Alex is forcing me to see. I'm just a little nervous about it, that's all.'

'Oh, right right! That is today. That man should really leave you alone after all the harm he's done to you. Don't worry child, he will have to pay the price for all his atrocities in front of Jesus someday.'

Life seemed so simple for Mrs. Rodriguez, thought Annie. The solution to all her problems lay in the hands of Jesus. Only if it were that easy. Annie simply looked down at her tea and slowly took a sip of it.

'Would you like me to accompany you today, dear?'

'Oh No Aunty! That's extremely nice of you to offer, but I really don't want to cause any more trouble for you.'

Trouble might not be the right word but it's not completely wrong either. The night Annie walked out of her apartment which she shared with her soon to be ex-husband Alex, she had no idea where to go. Annie did not have any friends in this city and the only place she ever went to was the church. That's when she thought of Mrs. Rodriguez. After all Mrs. Rodriguez lived alone and maybe Annie could crash at her place for a couple of nights before figuring out what to do next. So Annie was at Mrs. Rodriguez's door on that horrible rainy night all drenched and cold with a bag over her shoulder and some stitches on her forehead trying hard to control her tears. Mrs. Rodriguez invited her inside with so much love that she felt like a huge warm blanket was wrapped around her and nothing bad could happen to her as long as she was inside this blanket. Mrs. Rodriguez made her a hot cup of tea and made her eat some food and after hearing what had happened without even a second's hesitation, Mrs. Rodriguez took Annie's hand in hers and told her, 'Annie dear, you can think of this place as your own home. I've always thought of you as my daughter since the day we first talked. You are a gentle and kind soul and you do not deserve what happened to you. Please feel free to stay here as long as you want.'

Annie burst into tears at the affection a bare stranger was showing her. Since Annie wasn't working and hence did not have any money to pay her share of rent, she told Mrs. Rodriguez that she would love to help around the house with all the chores and would be more than happy to cook for her and take care of her. Mrs. Rodriguez denied it at first, but Annie insisted and finally she said 'As you wish, dear. But I'm glad that I'm no longer alone here. Now I got you.'

Chapter-6

Ahaana

In a different part of Mumbai Ahaana began her day in her tiny 1 BHK apartment close to her clinic but far enough from her home. Her friend Rahul had asked her a few days back if she could accommodate a new patient. Ahaana was already working round the clock and barely had any time to herself but being the hustler that she was she accepted the request also because it seemed like a sensitive case from whatever brief she had been given. Dr. Ahaana Khanna was a practicing psychiatrist now, well at least not officially. She was in her final years of completing her MD in Psychiatry and was already starting to make her way in the world of medical sciences of the mind. Despite having classes to attend, rounds in the hospital to get to, with barely having enough time to catch a lunch break or a breakfast bite, Ahaana also started taking up a few cases on her own outside the hospital. 'She lives to work', 'maybe she's after the money', 'she's always in a crappy attitude', 'Ugh, I cannot take how arrogant she is', 'she's so grumpy', 'she thinks she's better than us', 'she's only getting by because of that face' these were a few of the decorative comments that tagged along Ahaana in her hospital and college, duly given to her by her peers. True, Ahaana had always been a hardworking student since school, but now it was as if a new breed of workaholic maniac had been unlocked inside her. One might think that she'll lose it any day now if she kept up at this speed. No day offs, barely eating her meals, limited hours of sleep. But despite all this Ahaana only focused on her work going forward stronger if that was even possible. It's not like she didn't know what people were talking about her behind her back. But what did they know about her? About how her life had taken a turn for the worst all because of a choice she made, a choice she believed to be the right one. Therefore, hustling is not just a fancy word for her to make herself feel 'worthy' or to 'prove' something to somebody. She needs the work to support herself, to put herself through this last stretch of medical school. It does help that she loves what she does and is brilliant at it. Once her hospital shifts and classes for the day are over, Ahaana goes to her clinic, which was a tiny space with two rooms, only a few square meters bigger than her apartment, where she is the receptionist and the doctor. The place is well lit and Ahaana did her best to tidy up the place with whatever she could manage and now it looks way better than the building itself. Initially she had to pay out of her pocket just to afford the electricity bill alone as the owner of the building was fortunately kind enough to let her use the space rent free for the first 3 months.

Although the first month was scary for her, one being working 'unofficially' and second, losing sleep over how she will manage to take care of herself financially, things started gaining momentum when Ahaana got her first client who was the CEO of a very successful startup in Bangalore. The CEO apparently couldn't afford to make headlines in news regarding his 'mental health' as it would affect his stock prices and going to any renowned doctors in this city that only valued fame and glam would exactly do that. They would sell him out for free PR. Also, he wanted somebody who was young and could resonate with the problems of today rather than someone who's been warming up that couch for the last 30 years and who's best advice to him could be 'take a deep breath' or the occasional 'hmm' or nod of the head. The moment this CEO stepped foot through Ahaana's doors, her luck had stroked her again and tenfold this time. The thing with rich people is that everybody knows everybody in their tight knit circle, therefore word got around faster than Mumbai getting filled with actors and Ahaana's private clinic soon became the new hot spot for celebrities and VIPs who preferred a 'discreet' consultation. And boy, was she very good at what she did. Most of them only wanted to talk about their millionaire problems or needed anti-anxiety drugs which was not exactly what Ahaana had in mind when choosing psychiatry as a career choice.

She wanted to work with criminals in government facilities whose brain chemistry had been altered beyond anybody's imagination and to help normal people understand that anxiety and depression are very much 'real' issues as is a persistent cold or a fever. She loved to work on complex cases which would give her deeper level insights into the ever twisted, ever changing human mind holding a myriad of secrets still unknown to the universe and to us. But what she had going on now with her celebrity clientele was minting money for her. And until she graduated, this was the best possible option for her.

It was during this time that Ahaana was referred to Annie's case by a friend. After hearing almost the exact same issues from her regular clients', Annie's case offered her a chance to work on something real and different. Also, the fact that her soon to be ex-husband was the one paying for all their sessions made her even more curious to know what was going on here. So even with a tight schedule, Ahaana decided to take on Annie's case.

The appointment was scheduled for 10 AM and Ahaana was before time as usual. She walked into her office, checked her appointments for the day, tidied up the place and settled in her couch with her notepad and a pen, ready and excited to begin on a fresh note today. It was 10 minutes past 10 and while Ahaana was starting to lose hope that Annie might not show up, she heard a muffled low knock on her door. At first, she was not even sure if she heard it. Then she heard it again properly this time.

'Hi please come in' said Ahaana, really curious at this point to see Annie.

Annie twisted the handle and opened the door and took a step inside. She was wearing one of her faded out black and cream cotton saree, which was neither looking fresh nor ironed. Her hair was tied up in a loose rough bun and and she was tall and slender, actually a little too thin for her age. She was only a couple of years younger than Ahaana which was probably why the most striking thing about Annie that caught Ahaana's attention was her face. It was a beautiful face hidden beneath a lot of trauma and on the verge of premature ageing. Her lips were dry and a little washed out and pale, hollow cheeks and ashen complexion giving way to dark bags under her eyes. And it was at that exact moment when Annie's eyes shot up, looking straight at Ahaana. Ahaana knew that those were the eyes of a fighter. This young girl had endured a lot in such a short time and she's been running away from her demons all this time but those eyes had something hidden in them. Ahaana knew that unlike her usual cases Annie was different, this is not going to be another walk in the park. This time she will need to uncover a lot of skeletons in the closet and something told her that it was not going to be a pleasant ride.

Chapter - 7

Vihaan

The alarm went off at a low volume at 5:30 AM and Vihaan opened his eyes slowly. He had a lovely home situated in one of the poshest parts of this IT hub but what made it exquisite was the fact that it was close to the city but also had an incredible merge with nature too. He always loved spending time with nature even as a kid. Young Vihaan always looked forward to spending his summer and winter holidays in his family's farmhouse in the outskirts of Mumbai where there were orchids and vegetable gardens and squirrels and mud. It was an old colonial style house built during the rule of the British and has been in their family ever since he could remember. He never skipped a sunrise or a sunset from such a young age, a habit that he continues even today. This is specifically why he bought his current apartment even though it was expensive because he loved coming home to trees and sunshine at his backyard and not the same concrete jungle that he would look at for the next 16 hours from his office. Vihaan got up from the bed half dressed in his pants and shirtless and made his way to the kitchen to make his morning coffee. He was tall and ripped and had just hit 30. He had a successful multimillion-dollar company to run and who devoted more than half of his time at work because that was his world until he met her and that's when he also learned how to live. When he came back to his room with a steaming cup of coffee in his hand it was just in time for sunrise. He pulled back the curtains masking the gigantic French windows in his bedroom to let the first rays of morning hit his face and as he turned around he couldn't help but smile at the sight of a beautiful Helen sleeping in his bed completely and blissfully unaware of her admirer. He watched as the soft golden rays stroked her face and watched her glow in the morning light. This is also another reason why he loves to wake up early in the morning before her because he loves to watch her sleep. It's the most peaceful sight ever. He wanted to climb back into the bed and wake her up with a morning kiss but No, he couldn't break her out of her sleeping spell just yet. Its mornings like this that started adding more meaning to his life. As he took the first sip of his coffee watching his sleeping beauty he thought about the first time they met each other. Had he known that one day she would be the one he started his mornings and ended his days with? No. But did he wish that he could spend whatever time he had left in this world to just watch her simply exist? Hell yes !

Vihaan met Helen at his company's success party 2 years ago in Bangalore. This company was Vihaan's brainchild and to reach the kind of success that he had at such a young age was spectacular. He was a young passionate App developer who had the most crazy and unique ideas and he brought them to life only for the world to love them even more. A US firm had offered to buy their latest app and it was a deal that would open so many doors for him and his company. Vihaan was a firm believer that working is no fun if you don't occasionally enjoy the small milestones too. The office party was hosted in a five star hotel that had recently opened on the far end of the city and it was mostly for his colleagues and their partners only. Vihaan couldn't really focus on partying because as the founder and CEO he was still planning his next couple of months for his new upcoming projects and was starting to feel a little bored at his own party while everybody else seemed to be having a blast when all of a sudden he noticed a girl looking equally or possibly even more bored sitting at a far corner with a glass in hand. It looked like she was searching for someone in the crowd and was starting to get a little impatient. She definitely did not belong to his company which can only mean that she's here with someone who worked for him. She was wearing a black bodycon dress and high heels and had brown hair and was looking like a lost gem in a sea of grey shadows. Vihaan had his fair share of girlfriends in the past, and he had even dated a model for 2 months when he was in America but he never felt such a strong pull towards anyone like this before. There was an air of mystery surrounding her. She had a great physique and chose to wear something that showed off her silhouette but not in a vulgar way. It was the kind of dress that left you wanting more, imagining more. He slowly moved through the crowd not taking his eyes off of her even for a second, not even when someone spilled their drink on his white shirt because she was too important to miss over something trivial as a spoiled shirt.

'Hi', said Vihaan. He's always been a good conversationalist and smooth talking to a girl came naturally to him and it was also something that he secretly prided in.

'Hi…' said the girl in a slightly confused tone, sizing up Vihaan in a quick glace head to toe and her eyes lingering on the stain on his shirt for an extra second.

'I don't think I've seen you around at the office. Are you new here?'

'I don't work here'

'Oh! I see, Are you here with somebody then?'

'Yes'

OK! Not so much of a talker. Vihaan was used to girls throwing themselves at him and here was a girl that he was attracted to for the first time but she looked like she couldn't wait to get away from him fast enough.

'Cool party huh?!'

'What a bunch of 30 year old's trying hard to act like they are 18 again? No thank you.'

'Wow!!' after all those compliments that he's been receiving about what a great party it was, this girl has verbally slapped him and put him in his place with one simple sentence. 'Well, if this isn't really your scene, then why are you here?'

'I'm here with my friend.'

'Friend or boyfriend? Because that guy's got some nerve leaving a beautiful lady alone in a place like this?' Her next answer would be the key to knowing if she's single or even interested in Vihaan.

'You'd really fit in well with rest of the nosy aunties in my neighborhood. And what's wrong if I am alone? It's a lame party not murder club.' Definitely not the reply Vihaan was expecting, but he could just feel the heat rise up. He could not get enough of her.

'Haha… I'm sorry for being nosy but you looked like you were searching for someone in the room.'

'So exactly for how long have you been watching me Mr. Nosy or should I rather say stalker?'

She is bouncing off each of his questions with counter questions that is starting to make him look like a creep.

'Well can't say exactly because I lost track of time since the moment I laid my eyes on you'

'That is your pickup line? Really?'

Okay he's officially blowing this. It's the first time while flirting with a girl that he managed to make her feel disgusted instead of sexy. His game is falling apart miserably and only a miracle can save him now.

'Too cheesy for your taste?'

She gave him a disapproving look and said, 'Listen I think I'm done here. I have to go now'

No no no! This is not how it was supposed to go down. He racked his brain to come up with something interesting to say to her and make her stay. He cannot let her get away. Forget her number he doesn't even know her name. How is he ever going to find her if she leaves? A year and a half ago Vihaan had been put in a really tough spot during his first investor's meeting where the potential investors were firing questions at him but Vihaan had tackled those questions like a pro even when he was not. He was smart enough to build and run this successful company at 28, what is going wrong when he's trying to impress this mystery girl? As he stood there with his train of thoughts, he helplessly watched her walk away.

'Hey man whatsup? You look like you lost something', it was Vihaan's best friend Sid who came looking for him. Unlike Vihaan, Sid was having the time of his life. And judging by his condition, Vihaan was not sure how this guy was going to make it home.

'I did lose something. I met this amazing girl and I let her get away.'

'Is Vihaan Khanna whining over a girl? Let her go man you'll get a dozen of them. This is the city of angels.'

'No, you don't get it dude. She's not some girl. I felt this strange pull towards her like a spark, like I needed her.'

Sid looked at him with a straight face, 'Ah! I see what the problem is, it's been like what? 2 hours? And you're still sober. Let me get you a drink and you'll be good as new.'

'Nope. Can't drink. I have to drive back home.'

'What is wrong with you? This is your party. Why didn't you take an Uber like everybody else?'

'Guess I didn't think it through. But hey I am hungry so let's get something to eat?'

'You don't need to ask me twice. Come on bro.'

As Vihaan was being led through the crowd by Sid, he couldn't help but scan the room as far as his eyes would go in the darkness searching for her, but it looked like she simply vanished into thin air.

It was way past midnight now and almost everyone had left the party and Vihaan was about to leave as well when he noticed someone standing on the balcony of the hall facing the skyline. It was a chilly winter night and even with his jacket Vihaan paused for a second as he set foot on the balcony when a cold crisp breeze stroked his face. It was a girl and as he moved closer to her he noticed that she was wearing a black bodycon dress. His heart skipped a beat. It was her! He had wound up at last with his mystery girl. Miracles do happen!

Vihaan never believed in second chances until now. He walked towards her and noticed that she was shivering so badly being out in the cold. He felt concerned and was about to take off his jacket but he paused for a second because he did not want to come across as some pervert trying to grab a girl from the back. So, he took a few steps forward and stood next to her.

'Hey! We meet again'

Her eyes shot up at Vihaan startled to hear a voice as she was focused on her phone with a worried expression on her face.

'Oh my god! You scared me!'

'I'm sorry I didn't mean to scare you. What are you still doing here?'

'What do you mean?'

'The party is over and everyone left. Are you still waiting for your friend or maybe can I help…'

'Listen dude, it was nice talking to you earlier but please leave me alone', she was clearly pissed off at him and probably thought that he was trying to hit on her when in reality he was actually feeling extremely concerned for her because the place was almost empty except for some workers who had come to clean up the place and Vihaan noticed a few of them already eyeing her from a distance. He didn't need to think hard to know what was probably going on in their head by the way they were checking her out from the back. One of them was lingering around the balcony until he saw Vihaan walk towards her.

'I'm not that kind of a person. You're getting the wrong...'

'Then what kind of a person are you? You've been following me the whole time.'

'I did not follow you, I happened to notice you.'

'Yeah right. Now please leave me alone.'

Vihaan was starting to feel a little bad now. He understands that she is only trying to protect herself from a total stranger and he can't blame her for being so rude to him because this society has forced women to walk around while holding up their toughest armor. But no matter what, he is not leaving her alone here now and that's final. Clearly she is not aware of the other set of 'eyes' on her.

'Listen ma'am, I cannot leave you alone here.'

'Why not?'

'Because.... Because its late and it's not safe here to be alone.'

'Yeah I blame the one who decided to host an office party in this remote no network area.'

'I'm sorry I didn't know about that.'

'Why are you apologizing? It should be your boss who should apologize.'

'Um... I am the Boss!'

Vihaan saw confusion turn into recognition and recognition turn into shock on her face.

'Wait... you are Vihaan Khanna? Founder of CloudZen? Oh! I remember seeing that feature on the news about you. That's why I thought you looked familiar earlier. Wait, so this was your company's success party?'

Vihaan smiled at her and said, 'Okay slow down. And yes, this is my party. I swear I had no idea it would turn out to be a lame party for some silly 30-year olds. Sorry about that.'

She seemed relieved to know now that he was not some creep. But he saw her change her demeanor quickly.

'I'm sorry for being rude to you earlier. And sorry about what I said about your party. I was a little frustrated at my friend who ditched me. But please don't worry about me. I can get myself home safely.'

And her armor is back up again. But in a way he liked it because she did not throw herself at him just because she got to know that he was rich now.

'I'm sorry but I cannot leave until I've made sure that the last person has safely left my party. Now please tell me who did you come here with so that I can inform them that they forgot something important.' Even as he said this part of him was feeling sad about the fact that there is a possibility that she might end up being one of his employees' girlfriend. But her safety was his prime concern at the moment.

'I came here with Natasha. She insisted that I tag along for the party.'

'Oh Natty!' relief washed over Vihaan knowing that she was here with her girlfriend and not a guy 'No worries. I'll call her right away.'

'No don't call her' she held Vihaan's hand to stop him from calling Natasha. Vihaan looked at her questioningly.

'When you came to talk to me earlier I was searching for her. I found her later making out with a guy. I can only assume it was Sid because she's been crushing on him since forever and that's the whole reason she wanted to go to this party in the first place because she could meet him outside of office. I waited for her to be done to go home but she told me that she'll be going home with him instead.'

Vihaan knew that Sid had more to him than just being his legal advisor and best friend. He never felt more thankful to Sid.

'Um.. okay!' Vihaan couldn't help but smile at the whole side story that had just come to light.

'Yeah, I've been stood up and when I'm not even on a date. But don't worry about it. I'll call an Uber.' She lifted her phone up for Vihaan to see. But the screen was pitch black.

'Did your phone just die?'

'What?' she started tapping on her phone relentlessly but with no use. 'No no no! This cannot be happening!'

He could see her face getting pale and scared and clearly, she was calculating her next best options.

'Now can I drop you home, please?'

She looked at him contemplating her next move. She still didn't trust him fully and it was written all over her face.

'I won't try to hit on you with anymore cheesy lines. I promise.'

She smiled at that. It was the first time he saw her smile. If he thought she couldn't be more beautiful he was wrong. She had the kind of smile that put a thousand stars to shame.

'So, shall we Ma'am.'

'You can call me Helen'

'Nice to meet you Helen.'

'Nice to meet you too Vihaan.'

He noticed that she was shivering even more now and he immediately took off his jacket and wrapped it around her. If it was not his eyes deceiving him he saw her cheeks turn pink while tucking a loose strand of hair behind her ears, as they locked eyes for what seemed like the longest minute. Standing under the stars, overlooking the Garden City, on a balcony with the girl of his dreams and his heart beating fast enough to drown out every other noise, worry and concern, Vihaan felt like his story was just beginning.

It is rare to witness rain on a chilly winter evening in Bangalore, but when the evening itself was starting off to become a rare chapter in Vihaan's life, the rain seemed to fit in perfectly and made his drive with Helen an unforgettable one. Vihaan was glad that he had cleaned his car right before he left for the party because he was definitely not expecting a woman, and such a beautiful one too, to be his passenger princess the following evening. Women tend to judge a man's character based on how well kept his home is and sometimes his car too! Usually, it was Sid who took up the passenger seat and whenever he did, he always made sure to leave stains of soft drinks or coffee on the seat. So, luck really was on Vihaan's side tonight. He noticed that Helen was still preoccupied with something on her mind, even amidst the pitter patter of the rain he could hear her occasional heaved breathing.

'Hey, you alright?'

'....'

'Helen?'

'Huh?... I'm sorry, were you talking to me?'

'Um... considering the fact that it's only the two of us in here, I guess I am. You seem distressed. Are you okay?'

'Yes. It's just that... oh my god this is even embarrassing to say.'

'Wait what happened? Did I do something?'

'No no its not you. I'm getting this weird car smell like somebody ate something in here and it is making me a little nauseous.'

Bloody Sid! It totally skipped his mind that the previous night he was out with Sid and he was nagging Vihaan to get fish sticks which was apparently the new hip thing that had come up in the city. That idiot!

'I'm so sorry. You know Sid tends to eat and drink a lot in here and even though I deep cleaned the car just yesterday I guess the smell didn't get out completely.'

'Yeah that must be it. Did he eat fish in here by any chance?'

'Ah! Yes. Funny story actually, yesterday after work Sid and I hit up this new spot where they serve food in the car and he was hell bent on getting their signature fish sticks. So, it's basically fried fish which is marinated in this spicy sauce which is really tasty and....'

Vihaan glanced over towards Helen while speaking and he was shocked to see that her face had turned pale and she was covering her mouth with one hand, just seconds away from throwing up. What was an interesting story for him was starting to make Helen sick. Poor thing was trying so hard not to throw up in the car. Vihaan pulled over immediately and since it was way over midnight now, the streets were almost empty except for a street vendor on the side of the street. He turned to get a good look at her.

'Helen? Oh my God! Are you okay?'

'I'm fine' her voice did not sound fine.

'Okay let's get some fresh air. Come on'

'But it's raining'

'Not an issue.'

Vihaan always had an umbrella in his car just because Bangalore weather was so unpredictable and he too inherited his family's OCD genes a little. The rain had calmed down to a pleasant drizzle now. But the streets were foggy and the temperature had dropped by a couple of degrees.

Vihaan got out of the car, went over and opened the door for Helen, and as if on cue, she got out and made a beeline towards a huge tree on the side of the road adjacent to the pavement. Vihaan followed her. She couldn't hold it in any longer and started vomiting behind the tree. It was probably a second later when she felt her hair being pulled away from her face. Once she was done, and turned to face Vihaan, he noticed that she couldn't bring herself to look him in the eye. She is so cute, he thought.

'Hey are you ok? Feeling better now?'

She somehow managed to look up at him. 'Yeah, I am feeling a lot better. And....I'm sorry you had to see that.'

'Seriously? If anybody should be apologizing it should be me for letting my friend stink up my car like that.'

'Please don't mention the smell or fish again because I can feel it coming right back.'

'Oops yes sorry! You know what, I might be able to make u feel better. Come on.'

He got his jacket from the car, wrapped it around her and led her towards the street vendor a couple of feet away from their car. The vendor had a tiny roof made of sheet pulled over the stall and the whole place was empty except for the two of them. Vihaan asked her to sit down and went to the vendor.

Helen had no clue what was happening. 5 mins later Vihaan was back with 2 cups of lemon tea and a lemon for her to keep in her hand.

'Here, have some of this slowly and this lime is for the rest of our ride, try to smell it every now and then and you won't feel nauseous again.'

Helen couldn't help but smile. Vihaan sat next to her. The scene unfolded like an excerpt from an old Bollywood movie. Foggy and empty streets drizzling with rain, a tea shop on the side of the road with a couple sitting next to each other sipping piping hot tea.

'Hey, thank you' said Helen.

'No mention. You feeling okay now?'

'Much better', and as she said this Vihaan noticed the color rushing back to her face or was she blushing again? She seemed to be getting prettier with every passing moment. The soft warm glow of the street light hitting her face just right, softening her cheeks and making her eyes twinkle, started getting Vihaan's heart racing again. He was tempted to pull her close and kiss her, but if he did that, he might be demoted from a creep to a pervert! No. He had to stay calm besides he was in the most magical hour of his entire existence with this girl and he wished for that night to never end.

'Vihaan?'

His name sounded sweeter on her lips. He didn't realize that he had such a handsome name until he heard her call it out.

'Yeah?' he responded.

'When I got sick earlier, you didn't even hesitate for a moment, you just knew what to do and this tea is making me feel so good already. Did you have to take care of a lot of drunk girlfriends?'

Vihaan couldn't help but laugh at that last question. She really does think he was some kind of Casanova.

'Well, no, I did not have to take care of a lot of drunk girlfriends, although if that were the case I would've done the same anyway. It's my sister actually. She used to get car sick all the time as a kid and gradually I learned how to take care of her whenever that happened.'

'Wow! So, u have a sister, got any other siblings?'

'No, its just me and her' Vihaan's tone changed and he started getting a little quiet as the conversation moved towards his sister.

'What's her name? And what does she do?'

'Well… um.. her name is Ahaana and …' Vihaan took a moment to clear his throat, 'I actually don't know where she is or what she is doing right now'

'Why? I'm sorry if I'm overstepping here but did something happen?'

'It's a long story and it was a long time ago, I haven't thought about it in a while or even talked about her.'

'Did she get involved with something bad?'

'No, no, nothing like that. Ahaana was the smartest one between the two of us. Always excelled in her academics, was the perfect daughter and an even better sister. She's five years older than me and I meant the world to her. She'd really do anything to make me happy I just wish she didn't choose a guy she knew for some time over her family.'

'Don't tell me your family disowned her for loving someone.'

'She chose to leave us and go start a life with him. My father is a very proud man and he did not call her back when she stepped out of the house on that horrible night. My mother was crying a lot. I remember getting so pissed off at her and I was too young to understand these things back then. You could say I was an overprotective brother. I sided with Papa and told her strictly not to leave. But she had already made up her mind. And out she went. That was the last time we saw her.'

'Wow, that's heavy, I'm really sorry for bringing it up. But I think if you guys maybe tried to understand her a little bit more, maybe tried convincing her in a gentler manner, she might've been more reasonable.'

'I guess. But we'll never know now. Nothing felt the same after she left. I lost my best friend and my sister. And I hated spending every second in that house because my parents never talked about her again. I decided that I needed to move far away from all this. Found a course that I liked in the US and didn't think twice.'

'I can only imagine how difficult it must've been for you. I mean parents they come from a different generation but why did you not try to reach out to her again?'

'I don't know…'

'I think you do know. You really seem to miss her.'

'I've never really talked about this to anyone. Not even Sid. Losing her felt like losing a part of me.'

Vihaan felt Helen holding his hand.

'Hey it's okay. It's still not too late to think about it.'

'Yeah I guess. Thank you for listening.'

'No problem! And I think we should get going now.'

Vihaan and Helen got back into the car. It was almost 1 am when Vihaan dropped her at her apartment.

'Well, thank you for the ride Vihaan. It was a real pleasure meeting you.'

'The pleasure was all mine' smiled Vihaan.

Helen got out of the car still wearing Vihaan's jacket and right before she reached the gate she realized it and rushed back towards him to return it.

'I can be so silly sometimes. Here's your jacket.'

'It's still cold out here, you keep it and maybe you can return it to me tomorrow.'

'Tomorrow?'

'I'd love to take you out for coffee tomorrow, if you'd be okay with that', Vihaan smiled at her. Even though he was acting so cool on the outside he was wishing so badly that she'd say Yes to him.

'Vihaan Khanna are you asking me out on a date?' asked Helen with a smile playing on her lips.

'Yes I am.' Said Vihaan smiling back at her.

He looked at her with all the longing he had been trying to hide all night. He never wants to forget this moment with her.

'Yes I am asking you out on a date.'

Helen didn't say anything and walked towards the gate. Vihaan's heart sank. He really thought they had a spark, a connection. He could feel it in his bones.

He saw her pause mid-stride. She turned to look at him. She was smiling again.

'Pick me up at 5:00 tomorrow. You know where I live.' It took a second for him to process the fact that she just said yes to go on a date with him. Vihaan was bursting with happiness. What started out as a very boring night had just altered the course of Vihaan's life forever. He knew this was only the beginning of their story.

Chapter- 8

Sometime in 1999

What goes on in a 10-year-old girl's head cannot be precisely comprehended by anyone, even if the person in question is a parent themselves. They say children are like sponges and they tend to absorb whatever their environment lets them consume. What if some things are beyond what their environment feeds them? What if someone is born to be bad? Can you really stop them?

The night was calm, almost ominously silent for what was about to happen in a matter of hours. When it was almost midnight, a window cracked open slightly in one of the houses and a little girl slipped out into the night, quiet like a cat. The waist high shrubs helped conceal a 10-year old's petite figure easily. Eyes filled with determination she made her way through the shadows towards her neighbor's house. She knew that one of the fences was broken and can be easily detached. She was careful to keep the noise down and very slowly she detached the loose fence and stepped *foot in the neighbor's property. There were no lights inside the house. Good!*

She quietly walked towards the backside of the house where the kennel was and there he is. Johnny, the neighbor's Pitbull which they could never stop talking about. It was always who Johnny liked the most in the Sharma household, what was his favorite toy, what he ate and not ate. They bought one expensive breed of dog and suddenly they were experts in dogs. The neighbors were starting to get tired of the Sharma's constant boasting and show offs.

You can fool people but you cannot fool a dog because at the slightest sound of a dry leaf crunching under her feet, Johnny was awake and barked at her a couple of times. But she had anticipated that and moved closer to him to let him get a whiff off of her, so that he'll know that she's not the enemy. She was whispering now, 'Hey Johnny, you want a snack?' She revealed a banana that had been concealed inside her pockets. Johnny loved bananas and since the Sharmas thought it was getting him fat, they had put him on a diet where bananas where strictly avoided. This, was again, another piece of public information because even if the other parents in the neighborhood were unaware of their own children's food habits the Sharmas made sure that the whole neighborhood knew about Johnny's complete diet plan. Johnny's eyes lit up at the sight and smell of the banana and he started wagging his tail excited to munch on his unexpected midnight treat.

'Oh, you want this? Okay boy here, get it', she got him excited by dangling the snack in front of his eyes and once she knew he was ready, she slipped him the banana.

Johnny lunged forward, devouring his favorite snack. In a matter of seconds, he finished eating it and now she waited.

He was walking around normally at first and it might have been close to a minute when it looked like something caught in his throat. He wanted to choke or throw up but his feet gave away under his body first. She watched, her eyes gleaming with satisfaction in the moonlight as Johnny fell on to the ground, his body shaking violently. He could not bark anymore only tiny whimpering sounds escaped his helpless lips. As his body started paralyzing, he was looking at her now, the only other living being at his proximity, who was in capacity to help him. Yet we think that dogs cannot be fooled. Her 10-year-old brain thought that Johnny was a stupid dog because he did not smell the rat poison tablets that she had inserted inside the banana earlier. A mix of white foam and blood started forming around Johnny's mouth. He was throwing up more blood now and just before life left his him, she walked towards his frantically shivering body, looked at his wide panic-stricken eyes and said in a low whisper 'That's what you get for biting kids. Now they don't have to be scared of you anymore. Goodbye Johnny'. Johnny's body stopped shaking and became lifeless. Once she was sure that he's dead, she moved closer to him, kneeling down and unhooking his collar. She retreated back into her house with Johnny's collar in one hand and tossing the banana peel in the compost pit.

The next morning, she woke up after a peaceful night of sleep to a lot of commotion outside. She sat at the breakfast table with her father who was immersed in his newspaper.

'Why are there so many people outside?'

'You know Johnny, the Sharma's new dog, it died last night.'

'Oh no! But what happened?'

'They are saying that he was poisoned probably. You know, ate some poisonous plant probably in the backyard.'

'I'm not surprised. It was becoming like a forest over there. I told you I was afraid to let the kids play at their place. They should've cleaned up that mess instead of talking about the dog all the time', pitched in her mother while she brought her daughter's breakfast and milk to the table.

'Well, I'm sure they regret not doing it now.' said her father going back to reading his newspaper.

'Oh, poor Johnny.'

She thought her breakfast was very delicious and finished it completely like a good girl and also to her mother's slight surprise and went on to watch her cartoon on TV just like her usual Saturday morning.

Chapter- 9

Ahaana

'Would you like to have something to go with your coffee ma'am? We have freshly restocked our signature cakes just now.'

'Oh! No, thank you. I'm good for now, I'm just... um, waiting for someone to arrive.'

'Sure ma'am. I'll come back later.'

Ahaana couldn't remember the last time she indulged in a cake. She couldn't even recollect the last time she was at a café waiting for someone. It is fascinating how much a person can change in 10 years and yet stay the same too. She used to be different, back in college she used to love skipping classes once in a while to sneak out with Zayyan to eat panipuris or go for a bike ride with him. There was a little shack in front of their college which was the students' main hub at that time and that's where he would always wait to meet her and take her out after classes. They loved enjoying chai and pakoras at the shack while it rained heavily outside. She missed the feeling of being slightly drenched in the rain, standing at a corner of the shack, huddled close to Zayyan and sipping a cup of piping hot tea and taking a tasty bite of the spicy pakoras. That place was not glass paneled or did not have cozy couches like this café does. This place looked great, straight out of Pinterest but just like any other café that's in every corner now. It looked like a place without a soul or a story. She really missed that old feeling and she realized that she missed him even more. Ahaana could feel her eyes starting to tear up. But, No. She cannot be weak now because she is about to meet her brother any minute now, after 10 years!

Ahaana looked at the latte art on her coffee. Oh yes, she switched to coffee now because tea was something she only started drinking ever since she met him and only with him. The café was pretty sparse as it was a working day and the usual crowd will only pull up a little later in the evening and she liked the calmness and made a mental note to take herself out like this once in a week because she's been a complete workaholic for the last few years and this little indulgence feels nice. Also, now she was successful and financially secure and honestly, she didn't even need to be at work so often. She was pretty famous now, like father, like daughter, and had 2 clinics of her own and people working for her. She is reaching heights that she was scared to even dream of once upon a time, but all that hard work has started paying off now.

She took a sip of her coffee when she heard the door open and a young handsome man in his late 20s, walked into the café. He was scanning the room and his eyes landed on her. She'd recognize his face anytime, anywhere! Ahaana silently gasped for a second. The last time she met him, he was still a kid figuring out his life and now there he is a young man. She was getting overwhelmed with emotions and felt a little sad that she never got to see him in his 20s. He must be 30 years old now.

Vihaan smiled and walked towards her and Ahaana could see tears starting to form in his eyes. She couldn't believe even as a grown-up he was still so emotional but that's what she always found so pure and innocent about him. Her little boy. He wrapped her in his arms and as much as Ahaana tried holding back her tears, she couldn't. After a moment, she asked him to sit.

'Hi', said Ahaana.

'Hi Didi', said Vihaan smiling now, 'How have you been?'

'I've been alright. Tell me about you. I read the feature about your company CloudZen. Congratulations to you.'

'Aaah its nothing.'

'No its not. Don't dismiss it like that. I always knew you'd make it big and look at you all so grown up now. I'm so happy for you.'

'Hello Ma'am, hello Sir, can I take your order please?' interrupted the waiter in between the sister brother reunion.

'Hi yes, one double chicken burger and milkshake for him' said Ahaana almost like a reflex.

Vihaan started laughing after hearing Ahaana's order.

'Didi no offense but I'm not a teenager anymore and I certainly don't have milkshakes n burgers now.'

Ahaana felt a little embarrassed. 'Right', she said, 'I don't know it was a force of habit I guess. Every time we went out you cried for your burgers and milkshakes said Ahaana sheepishly. 'So, what would you like to have now.'

Instead of answering to Ahaana, Vihaan replied directly to the waiter 'If you don't mind could you please come back after a little while. One more person might be joining us soon.'

'Sure, Sir no problem.' And the waiter left.

'I'm sorry, did I miss something,' asked Ahaana confused.

'No no, I probably should have told you before but I felt it was better if I did that in person.'

'Wait, don't tell me you're married and I missed your wedding!' Ahaana felt a pang in her chest and her face fell at the thought of missing out on her brother's wedding.

'Do you really think that I'll get married without you by my side? I know I haven't been in touch with you but that's really too much, even for me.'

'So, then who am I meeting?'

'She's my girlfriend. Her name is Helen.'

Ahaana's face lit up immediately. 'Wow!! That's interesting. What does she do?'

'She's a dancer and owns a small dance studio here. And she's the reason why we're here today. I mean, I missed you so much over the years but I was scared to reach out and when I talked to her about you, she encouraged me to contact you. So, basically what I'm trying to say is… um… I really love her, like a lot. We have been in a relationship for two years now and I'm actually thinking of proposing to her.'

'I see.' Ahaana just sat back, took a deep breath and took another sip of her coffee averting her eyes away from Vihaan.

'Didi yes I know how it looks. That day I too was against your relationship because back then I didn't care too much about these things. I was conditioned to think that it was a bad thing. Then you left. And I started discovering more about things I wanted to study and build a career on. Papa and I even had a big fallout too.'

'What?'

'Yeah. After you left things were never the same. Even though I took our parents' side that night, I wish now that I maybe should've tried to understand your side of things too. Maybe all of us could have reached sort of a middle ground maybe. Anyways, Papa started acting like I had to take your place somehow. He always wanted you to become a famous doctor like him but when you left, it was more than he could handle. He started imposing his dreams on me and not in a nice way. I felt suffocated in that house. We fought a lot.'

'What about Mom?'

'Mom started drinking more and staying out more with her clubs and kitty parties. I felt so lost and alone. There was no one I could talk to openly and I was going crazy. Things only got bad from there. I met some guys who started selling me weed and some other drugs and I'm not proud of it but that felt like my only escape at that point. It went on for a few months, and before I realized I was addicted to that stuff. Until one day when Papa caught me red handed using the substance. But that was one turning point where both Mom and Papa came together and decided to get me the help I needed. They put me in a rehab facility outside the city. It took me a while but I came back sober after a few months and few days later Papa told me that he wouldn't force me to take up a career that I didn't want and that he'll support me in whatever I wanted to do. So, I told him that I was always interested in app development and I wanted to study in this university in San Francisco. He agreed and when I attempted for a scholarship, I actually got in. That was like an assurance to Papa that I was serious about this stuff and that's how I left for America.'

'I'm so sorry to hear that Vihaan. God! You must have hated me so much. I had no idea that me leaving would create so much disturbance in the house.'

'Actually, it was quite the opposite. Those few years at home made me realize that you've been taking these bullets for me. I never had to deal with the pressure of fulfilling Papa's dreams. Never had to look perfect for our Mom. But you were all of that and you seemed to do it effortlessly too.'

Ahaana replied with a smile and asked, 'So, how was San Francisco?'

'Oh, it was like a breath of fresh air. I travelled, made a lot of friends but something still felt missing from my life. It was like a sense of purpose. I didn't want to come back home with nothing. So, with some guidance from my professors I developed an app at Uni which was showcased at one of the biggest tech expos in America. There were hundreds of candidates and if you got to be selected as the best tech at that expo, well you were sorted for a long time then.'

'And I guess your app was selected as the best?'

'Well not quite… it's even better. This huge company bought my app.'

'Wow! You really had to grow up in a short time kiddo.'

'Hahaha yeah.'

'So, I assume you met Helen after that?'

'Yes, and it was not an impulse thing to get into a relationship with her. She's very mature about these things actually.'

'Right.' Said Ahaana and Vihaan thought he sensed a little dismissal in her tone.

'Didi, I know what you must be thinking. I have dated before but I never felt so serious about anyone else in my life before. She grounded me, taught me to see the world from a different light and motivates me to work hard and be the best version of myself. I don't know how to explain it but she's more mature than most girls I've met and she's got her own thing going on too, I love how ambitious she is. So, before anyone, I wanted your blessing for us and then I wish to take this forward with our family. But as you might have guessed now, there are a couple of issues at stake here. One, she's a Christian and second she's a year older than me.'

'Vihaan, listen, if after everything u saw me go through in my life and you still think that age and religion are things I consider as "issues", then you still don't know your sister. All I'm thinking is are you really sure about her? Do you know everything about her? Right now, you're head over heels for her and are you thinking of proposing to her just based on those emotions? What do we know about her family, her parents, where she's from?'

'Well I…' Vihaan was starting to reply when the door to the restaurant opened once again and walked in Helen.

'Hey babe. Over here.' Vihaan raised a hand and pointed her towards the direction to their table.

Helen walked towards the table smiling at Vihaan, but then her eyes rested on Ahaana and her smile faded. Ahaana felt a chill run down her spine. It was like she was having an episode of De ja vu. Because she was now looking at the same girl who walked into her tiny clinic 7 years ago who was on the verge of a divorce and had a weary, defeated look on her face and not a single cell in her body had the urge to live to see another day. She saw the same eyes of a fighter but her face was a little different now. It was a little younger and had more life to it. What does this mean? Ahaana felt her whole body go cold and shuddered when she realized that she had finally found her patient who was a murder suspect and vanished the face of the earth 7 years ago.

Chapter - 10

Annie

The idea of opening up about her trauma and bad marriage to a random person was not very appealing to Annie. But this doctor sitting across her did not seem like the judgmental kind. In fact, she almost thought that she saw empathy in her eyes. Or was it another tactic of these shrinks? Annie's overthinking had no bounds. For the first 3 sessions Annie didn't speak to Dr. Ahaana hoping that keeping mute might get her out of this arrangement easily but this doctor did not seem to be giving up that easily. Sometimes her prompts made Annie want to divulge everything about her life to her but she was afraid if the doctor knowing her past might complicate her divorce further. Every session was the same, where Dr. Ahaana would keep asking her to say something, anything really, and Annie would just sit there quietly.

Weeks passed and it was their fourth session, and Annie was being her usual quite self. After a few minutes of watching her Dr. Ahaana, let out a deep breath, sat up straight, removed her glasses and kept her writing pad and pen aside and said, 'Annie, I know that you are afraid of talking to me and honestly I would feel the same way too if I were in your place.' Nothing, Annie was still sitting quietly looking down at her hands. Dr. Ahaana continued, 'It is not easy being a woman, right? Everybody demands so much from us, we keep giving and giving and it's just not enough. It only gets worse when the people you once trusted with your life fails you at your weakest moments and then you're left to fight your own battles.' Again, nothing from Annie. 'But life is a tricky thing you know. Just when you think that it's going well, peacefully, it is at that exact moment when you least expect it, something goes terribly wrong. You know I was not supposed to be working here now, I should to be working for my PhD but what else can you do when your family disowns you?' Annie's eyes shot up at that last sentence. Dr. Ahaana continued, 'Do you know why did I even agree to talk to you Annie?'

Annie nodded to say a non-verbal 'No'. That was the first response Dr. Ahaana got in weeks. 'I read about you and all I could see was a strong woman. A strong woman who deserved the best, who fought for what she wanted but was completely wronged because of her life choices.'

'But it was not my choice! My parents forced me to marry Alex. I did not want to.' Burst out Annie, out loud with tears rolling down her cheeks now. Dr. Ahaana was quite for a moment. And then she asked, 'Why did your family force you to marry Alex?'

'Because he works in the city. My family felt that there was no way an alliance like that would ever find us again.'

'You did not like Alex?'

'No.'

'Why?'

'Because I didn't know him at all.'

'I understand. Arranged marriages can be scary. Were you given the chance to talk to him before even deciding on marriage?'

'No. You people don't understand! That is just not how things work in small towns. We do not have a choice. They decide and we have to listen.' Annie was shouting every sentence now. But Dr. Ahaana was used to this. Her years of training was not wasted.

'I see. Was there any other reason that you did not like Alex?'

'I was not ready to get married.' Annie said in a defeated voice now.

'Why were you not ready to get married?'

'I wanted to dance. Open my studio.' She said in a low voice as if saying her dream out loud might destroy it in a nanosecond.

'You are a dancer! That's really amazing. I don't see why that should stop after marriage.' Dr. Ahaana was trying to get more information on Annie's past now.

'You don't get it do you?' Annie looked up at again crying now.

Dr. Ahaana was a little taken aback by this.

'You people in your city lives with parents who get you everything to your doorstep will never know how much women like me have to struggle. In our village, they get young girls married off as early as when they turn 15. To them, we are just machines to make round rotis and take care of our husbands. I had to fight with my family so that they'll allow me to go to college. But how can you fight so much for each and every single thing you want? It drains you. And that's when I gave up hoping at least my husband would be better. Hoping maybe, just maybe my parents were right this time.' Annie let out a long sigh after this monologue.

'Annie, I'm extremely sorry to hear what you had to go through. Was Alex not the kind of husband you wished for? Did he hurt you?' Dr. Ahaana asked in a very empathetic tone. Annie wondered if that was also part of her training? To talk in such a cool and soothing voice like an emotionless robot.

'Well, not initially. He seemed very nice in the beginning. Bought me clothes and took me out for meals.' Annie was starting to sound normal now.

'Then what happened?'

'He said that we need to move to Mumbai because there were better job opportunities. What else can an unemployed wife do other than accompany her husband? So, I followed him here. He had promised that we'll live in a nice apartment and even promised to help me open my dance studio. But he brought me into a shit hole. Our apartment was nothing like what he promised, it was a shady neighborhood. And when I questioned him about it, he said that the broker had tricked him and promised that we'll move soon.

'I waited and a year passed by. One day I told him that it's okay if we cannot get a nice apartment but could I at least take dancing classes? I always wanted to have my own studio and teach dance. During the initial days of our marriage he seemed very supportive of my dreams.'

'What did he say to that?'

Annie looked up at Ahaana, there was a kind of bitter sweetness in her eyes

'He was smarter than I thought. A week later I found out that I was pregnant. So much for dreams.'

'But maybe having a baby could be a good sign no?'

'That's what I thought too. But that man is very cunning. He said, now that our family was about to become bigger, we had to save every penny we could and put the apartment idea on hold for a while.'

'I'm really sorry to hear that Annie.' Said Dr. Ahaana in her best apologetic tone. It was starting to sound very fake to Annie now.

'Are you really sorry doctor? Did you ever have to put your dream career on hold because life just started happening to you?' questioned Annie with angry eyes directed at the doctor.

'No, I did go after my career but I also lost a lot on the way.'

There was a brief silence in the room. But Ahaana wanted to keep the momentum going even if it meant breaking her rules a little bit and divulging bits and pieces of her personal information every now and then just enough to make Annie talk more. After all she seemed to trust Dr. Ahaana better when she talked about her personal traumas.

'What happened after the baby arrived?'

Ahaana noticed an immediate change of expression on Annie's face. As if her world just lit up thinking back to that time.

'Daisy is this perfect little girl. I was not the happiest person when I found out that I was pregnant initially but the moment I saw her, it was like a little angel telling me that everything will be alright. She was my angel.'

'That's really beautiful to hear Annie. How did Alex react to Daisy's arrival?'

At the mention of this, Ahaana noticed something change again in Annie, a slight quick tilt of the head to the right, as if she was snapping back from a dream.

'Alex? Huh being a father meant nothing to him. He started drinking more. He would shout at me for everything. Started coming home late and every time I questioned it we'd get into a fight.'

'I don't understand. Did he ever behave like this towards you before you were pregnant?'

'No.'

'Okay.... What happened after that?'

Annie started wrapping a small piece of the end her saree tightly around her finger. She started shaking and there were tears rolling down her cheeks now and in a cracked voice she said, 'He started having affairs with other women.'

'Are you sure about that Annie?' asked the doctor treading very lightly on this question.

'I saw it with my own eyes. How much more proof do I need? It was the worst night of my life. I asked him about her. He started lying. Nothing new about that right? But that night our arguments became a little too strong. He hit me. I said I cannot live with him anymore because he's a disgusting man. I grabbed Daisy and whatever I could and was about to leave when he tried to stop me and then...'

'And then? What happened Annie?'

Annie couldn't get the words out of her mouth. Ahaana waited. A few moments passed. Finally, Annie composed herself and said, 'It was raining heavily that night. The corridor outside our door was very wet and slippery. As I was about to walk out with Daisy in my arms, he grabbed my hand from the back, I slipped and... and right before I hit the floor I realized that Daisy was not in my arms anymore.'

A sharp gasp was heard from Ahaana followed by her clasping her hands over her mouth. Annie continued, 'When I woke up I was in a hospital. There is a little clinic in the neighborhood. He took me there because he said that I was bleeding. I asked him about Daisy. He said she fell from the first floor and had a lot of injuries and needed a lot of care but she'll be alright. I told him that I wanted to leave him and take our daughter with me. That I don't trust her with him. He said I cannot do that. Couple of days passed. This was the only thing I asked him which he kept denying. Once I knew that I was healed I ran away from the clinic.'

'But what about Daisy?' asked Ahaana.

'I couldn't take her with me. That's my only regret to this day. She needed medical care. Taking her would mean that I was risking her life dangerously. But I had made up my mind to go against him legally.'

'Where did you go that night?'

'To Mrs. Rodriguez. I met her in our church. She's the only one I knew in this city. I knew she'd help me.'

'You're still staying with her?'

'Yes.'

'Did you file for divorce?'

'Yes.'

'How did Alex react to that?'

'Why do you think I am here?' scoffed Annie.

'I don't understand.'

'Alex said he'll sign the divorce only under one condition that I needed to meet a psychiatrist. So, here I am.'

'But that doesn't make any sense'

'Nothing about my life ever made any sense doctor. Now can you help me or not?'

Chapter - 11

Ahaana

Ahaana lived in a really nice spacious new 2BHK apartment with a spectacular view of the city at night from her balcony. Now she could easily afford to move into an even bigger space, pretty much anywhere to her liking but what was the whole point when she had nobody to visit her anymore? Ahaana had a beautiful balcony too but she barely ever stood there or enjoyed the view. Her routine was simple and almost robotic. Her day started early to squeeze in a few minutes of yoga before grabbing a quick breakfast and heading to work. She is usually home by 6 and likes to cook her own dinner and rarely preferred take outs and eating out was an even rare event unless it was a working lunch or dinner. She catches up on new research papers in her field, while drinking her usual chamomile tea and is in bed by 10 PM, not a minute late. But today Ahaana could be seen sitting at the balcony, wrapped up in a blanket, looking quite disturbed. She had broken her routine, not even work stress had done that to her in all these years. Who cared about routine when her life was getting more chaotic with every passing day?

It was on nights like this that Ahaana let herself escape with thoughts of Zayyan. Being a doctor of the mind herself, she knew how toxic this was but she too was human after all. And humans did foolish things and had emotions and felt every feeling a little too much.

If high school was bad, then medical school was torture for Ahaana. But what wouldn't she give to go back there this very instant. Ahaana always attracted eyes wherever she went and medical school was no different. A lot of guys were swooning over her since the first day of college and even though she never entertained anyone among them she still somehow managed to earn more rumors than credits on her papers. Her father had tweaked the management's decision slightly to allow his daughter to get into the same college as him, to continue his legacy. But nothing stays a secret in college. This was the beginning of all the rumors and soon Ahaana realized that her fellow students saw her as an arrogant, rich girl who was only here because she was Daddy's little princess. Safe to say that Ahaana did not have a lot of friends in college but was still a popular person contrary to how she would have liked things to go.

She was a brilliant student and she was glad that at least her teachers could see her true self through her work and academics. Yet if there was something that bothered

Ahaana since day one, it was Zayyan. She hadn't been able to stop thinking about him since their first encounter. She thought there was a spark between them and it went both ways. But he seemed to be giving her mixed signals. Sometimes he acknowledged her presence by giving her a slight nod of the head and a little smile while passing each other in the hallways while at other times, when she tried approaching him in the hope of talking, he seemed to get away before she could even reach him. She knew he watched her from a distance but then why wouldn't he talk to her? Why keep this distance between them? He was a people's person after all. Professor's' favorite, juniors admired him, he had a huge circle of friends in every department and not to mention the number of girls who continued to propose to him even when he politely turned them all down. Did she say something wrong to him or offend him in some way? She waited a couple of months to see if things might improve between them or if he would at least like to be her friend? What if he too believed that she was a rich snob? Perfect! That would really be the icing on the cake.

One day Ahaana was going to the library a little late in the evening after classes and she overheard a couple of classmates talking about her.

'Bro are you seriously pursuing Ahaana Khanna? I know girls like her. First of all, she's totally out of your league and secondly she's will chew you up and spit you out once she's done with you.'

'That's bullshit, she's a quiet girl. There's no way she's like that.'

'Dude you're so naïve. She's already dated 4 guys in 2 months.'

'Okay... so? That doesn't mean anything.' Said the guy with a slightly faltering voice.

'Are you dumb? She dumped them after she got what she wanted from them. And it's not even that. I heard that she's sleeping with one of our professor's too. How do you think she's the topper in every subject? Come on she can't be that smart.' A few laughter could be heard following this remark. Ahaana knew that people did not like her but this was too much. She was really hurt to know this how people were seeing her. Who was making up these disgusting rumors about her? What did they even gain by slut shaming her? She was about to turn back and walk away when she heard a loud slap. She tried to see what was happening behind the library. She saw Zayyan towering over one her classmates who was on the floor a hand covering the side of the face where Zayyan had just hit him. She had never seen him so enraged. He was breathing hard and his face was red and fuming. He looked like a volcano about to erupt.

Zayyan grabbed the collar of the guy and pulled him up while the others started backing away. He was glaring at the guy like a predator about to rip apart his prey. 'If I hear any of you talking this way about Ahaana again, I won't stop at a slap.'

'But... but we didn't say anything about Ahaana.'

Zayyan slapped the guy once again.

'You're not even worthy enough to say her name with that filthy mouth of yours. Stay away from her. You get me?'

'Yes Sir!' said all of them in chorus like a bunch of scared nursery kids and scooted as soon as Zayyan relaxed his grip on the guy's shirt.

Ahaana felt exhilarated by what she had just witnessed. But this still doesn't prove anything. Zayyan could simply be a well-wisher or a good friend who simply reacted when he heard some guys talking ill about her. But one thing was for sure, her feelings for him had just intensified.

A week passed by when Zayyan continued to ignore Ahaana and she was sadly starting to feel like her next 4 years in college will be spent by just being acquaintances with the only guy for whom she had ever fallen for. Right before she went to her next class she remembered that one of her professors, Prof. Samuel had asked to meet her in his office. His office was in the new block and there was nobody else in the staff room when she walked in. Since Prof. Samuel was one of the senior professors, he had a cabin of his own. Ahaana felt a little strange walking into his empty office but she knocked and went in.

'Good Afternoon Sir, you asked to see me?'

'Oh yes dear. Please come in. Have a seat.'

She sat down on one of the chairs in front of him and simultaneously the professor got up and walked towards her and leaned on the table right in front of her. Ahaana felt a little weird at this proximity but she decided to keep quiet.

The professor looked at her intensely and said, 'You know that your papers for this coming exams will be checked by me where I will be allotting you the final marks.'

'Yes Sir, I understand that.'

'Good well you know, I could make things a little easier for you if you'd like.'

'I'm... I'm sorry Sir?' Ahaana cleared her throat, anticipating and afraid of what she was about to hear next.

'Well... its nothing new, we've had some great doctors pass out from this institution with exemplary results. Let's just say it was not all about hard work. We had a little secret. Sometimes working for your professor can make big changes in your results.'

'Are you asking me to work on a research paper Sir?' Ahaana was desperately hoping that was exactly what her professor was proposing.

'Oh dear Ahaana, so young, so naïve! No. I'm asking you to spend some time with me here after your classes.' He was touching her face now, 'you know a hardworking student like you deserves a break every now and then. I can help you relax, well we can both help each other have a good time and before you know it, your grades will be better than ever and you'll land that dream internship. You do know that a recommendation from me will get you into any top hospitals in this country right.'

Ahaana felt a wave of disgust engulf her. 'I'm sorry Sir.' Clearly this man did not deserve to be called 'Sir', but she tried to keep herself calm and get out of this situation in the safest way she could, 'I am not interested in whatever you're proposing. Now I need to get back to my classes.'

'I can also make life miserable for you here.' He grabbed her hand as she turned to go.

'Leave my hand.' Said Ahaana in a stern voice.

'What if I don't?' asked Prof. Samuel, tightening the grip around her wrist?

The answer came from the door, 'If you don't let her go now, then I'll be forced to show this video to the police and well, I don't have to explain what will happen to a well-respected man like you after that… Sir.' It was Zayyan standing at the door trying his best to not bash the old man's head on the table but Ahaana could see his body shaking with anger. Prof. Samuel did not expect that and realized that he had to stop now.

'Oh Zayyan, uh… its not like that.'

'Save it for the police. Ahaana, come with me.'

She had never been more relieved to see Zayyan. Once they were outside the building he took her to a café in front the college. It was nothing fancy, just a little shack which was the main hub of the students after classes. But since they were early, it was much less crowded and no other student in sight. Ahaana sat down at one of the tables on the side of the café while Zayyan came and sat next of her with 2 cups of steaming hot tea. He placed one cup infront of her 'Hey, you okay?' asked Zayyan in a genuinely concerned tone.

'Yeah… I guess.' Assured Ahaana.

'He won't bother you again if that's what you're worried about. I'll take care of that.'

'No, it's just… I was thinking what would have happened if you didn't walk in exactly when you did. It horrifying to think Prof. Samuel is such a disgusting man. I guess I got lucky you found me.'

Zayyan was quiet and Ahaana noticed that. She asked him, 'It was not a coincidence was it?'

Zayyan turned to look at her. His green eyes sparkling with a secret he's been hiding for a while now. 'No, it was not a coincidence.'

'How did you know where I was?'

'I asked your classmate Sruti.'

'Why would you ask Sruti where I was?'

'Because I didn't see you in class after lunch.'

'Why were you looking for me in class?'

'I like to watch you studying' admitted Zayyan in a shy low voice.

Ahaana couldn't help but smile at this.

'What?'

Zayyan sat back straight and turned to look at Ahaana. She could see the same spark in his eyes like the same one she saw in their first meeting. His mouth curled up with a smile and it seemed like he was about to let a big embarrassing secret out and Ahaana was all ears.

'Ahaana, I … I like you okay. I've liked you since the first day I saw you. That day when I helped you on your feet when you slipped and fell down in the rain, I never felt so clueless as to how to treat someone injured. And I've treated countless patients before. I'm actually pretty good with dealing with emergency cases too but when I saw you, all of my training failed me, I went completely blank and I don't know what was happening to me.'

'But you fixed my leg.'

'My mind blacked out but not my reflexes. It was a momentary thing and then I forced myself to focus and fix your leg. It was really hard to look away from your face.'

'Oh!' blushed Ahaana. 'But… why didn't you tell me this before? You always ignore me in the hallways. You never talk to me even when I tried talking to you. I thought you hated me.'

'What are you saying Ahaana? How could I hate you? It's complicated. We shouldn't even be having this conversation.' There he goes, back into his shell again. But she was not about to let him go now.

'No Zayyan, talk to me. What is it?'

'Because you're you and I'm just... me.'

'What do you mean?'

'Ahaana I don't want to date you, I want to build a life with you. I cannot bear the thought of seeing you with another guy. I wish to spend every waking moment with you. I like noticing every little thing that you do. I like watching you doodle, I like how organized you like everything to be, I feel sad every time I see you eating alone at the cafeteria, I like watching you eye that panipuri stall after classes but being scared to eat it because your father won't approve of it if he finds you there when he is around to pick you up. I admire how brave you are, always standing up for what feels right to you. And every time I see you in that white salwar, my heart beats faster than ever and I feel breathless, like I wanna hold you in my arms and kiss you.' Zayyan looked at Ahaana breathing faster now. That was the longest she'd ever heard him talk to her.

'What's stopping you then?' asked Ahaana in a soft voice.

'Because we're from different worlds, Ahaana. You don't get it. Everything about us, our backgrounds, our religion, our lives are polar opposites. If we go ahead with this it'll only create bigger problems for you and hurt you in the long run and I cannot stand to see you hurting because of me.'

'No, I know all of that Zayyan but how can you give up on something that you haven't even given a chance to? We're doctors after all, we are taught to not lose hope because anything can happen even during the last minute.'

He looked down at their hands. She was holding his hand now. He interlaced his fingers in hers, firm and confident. Zayyan looked deeply into Ahaana's eyes. His emerald green eyes were a tangled mess of sadness and bliss entwined. Like he's been searching for something all his life and now he finally found it. He moved a little closer to her and said, 'I love you Ahaana. You have no idea how badly I've wanted to say that to you.' Ahaana squeezed his hand in hers, giving him the only assurance he'll ever need, leaned in closer to him and said, 'And I love you too Zayyan.'

Chapter-12

Vihaan

VIHAAN: Hey!

HELEN: Hi!

VIHAAN: Coffee at 5? With me?

HELEN: That depends. Will you behave yourself?

VIHAAN: Yes Ma'am! I'll be a good boy.

HELEN: Still doubt it.

VIHAAN: Only one way to find out.

HELEN: You are very persistent.

VIHAAN: And you are very beautiful.

HELEN: Do you ever stop being so cheesy?

VIHAAN: Not with you.

HELEN: There is no escape is there?

VIHAAN: I'm afraid not.

HELEN: Guess I'll have to say Yes now.

VIHAAN: I promise you it'll be the best evening of your life.

HELEN: Hold your horses.

VIHAAN: Yes Ma'am. So, I'll pick you up at 5? ☺

HELEN: Yeah. I'll see you then.

After spending an unforgettable and possibly the best night of his entire existence with Helen after the office party, Vihaan knew he had to take this girl out on a proper date. The more she played hard to get the more he seems to be falling for her. But he couldn't stop thinking that she's trying to protect herself. He knows that she doesn't hate him now but why is she holding herself back so much? She prefers to be alone and do things on her own and is extremely independent and Vihaan can't help but think that maybe it's got something to do with a past. Yet, when she was with Vihaan that night, he noticed that a smile escaped her lips every now and then from her strictly controlled facial expressions. Whatever was holding her back, he knew that they can work on it together.

Vihaan reached her apartment at 5 on that chilly winter evening looking really sharp in his dark blue jeans and white turtleneck sweater that slightly hung loose around his muscular torso. The security guard wouldn't let him go inside so he texted Helen that he was waiting for her downstairs. As he watched the front door of the apartment building, there was a sudden gush of wind and walked out Helen, her dark brown hair let down loosely dancing with the breeze. She looked absolutely breathtaking in that loose fitting washed out blue jeans and a body fitting black sweater top with a dipping neckline and a black long jacket hanging in one hand. Vihaan felt like he forgot to breathe or even speak for a second. How could someone look so perfect in something so effortlessly simple? Vihaan felt like he was watching his own romantic movie unfold in front of him.

'Hi! You look beautiful', said Vihaan partially hoping that she won't take it as casual flirting because he really finds her so beautiful. To his relief she smiled and looked down and he thought he saw her blush and was trying to hide it with her open hair. 'Thank you! You look good too', Her first compliment! Vihaan thought this date was off to a great start already. 'Would you like to continue exchanging more compliments at the gate only or shall we head out for coffee?' teased Vihaan. Smiling, Helen replied, 'Let's go.'

It was a European themed café, with a fake fireplace and cozy interiors. They found a spot by the window in the far corner of the room, away from the noise and there was a table for two that looked like it was waiting for them to occupy. He pulled out her chair like a gentleman and sat down across her. They could see a park from the adjacent big window, children were playing, people had taken their dogs out for an evening walk, some were reading on the park bench and the street lights were just starting to turn on and that's when you could see that it was beginning to get colder outside as the air was looking very foggy. As they were waiting for their coffees to arrive Vihaan watched as the soft glow of the street light and the dim café lights added a warm glow to Helen's face. She looked calm and relaxed.

'What are you looking at?' asked Vihaan.

'The kids, at the park. Look how happy they are. Not a care in the world.'

'You like kids?'

'You don't?'

'Well, I haven't been around them much I guess. Besides they can be very unpredictable.'

'You create highly complex softwares for a living and you think kids are unpredictable?'

'Well, when you put it that way yeah it sounds pretty dumb. Programming is easy, if it's a yes, you go one way, if it's a no, you go the other way.'

'Kids are great. You just need to earn their trust and they'll become easier than computers.'

'You have a solution to everything' smiled Vihaan.

'Not exactly, I just don't give up that easily.'

'There we go, our first common trait. I too don't give up on anything that easily.'

'Yeah I figured that out earlier today'

'You know I was thinking of going back to America, maybe set up a headquarters there and get settled there. Bangalore was starting to feel a little tiring.'

'Why do I feel like you changed you mind?'

'Well, hearing you talk about those kids now, I realize that I never tried to connect with anyone or anything in this city on a deeper level. When I decided to move here, I was only weighing the pros and cons work wise. All of my decisions were made around how it might impact my work and the growth of my company. And even when I started living here, the only thing on my mind was my company.'

'So, you don't have any favorite places in this city?'

'Not really. I just go around with Sid. He's a big foodie and can be really nagging sometimes. How do you feel about Bangalore? ' asked Vihaan.

'I don't know, I feel really relaxed and easy living here. There's always something new on the horizon and people are nicer too.'

'In that case, I have one small surprise for you. I got us tickets to this theatre show happening in the city. I don't know much about art but when I asked around everybody said that it was an international dance company and apparently they are supposed to be really good' said Vihaan holding up two tickets in his hand.

Helen took the tickets from him and her eyes wide with surprise, 'No way!! The Enigma? It is my dream to watch their live show. But these tickets are really hard to get and must've been really expensive too right?'

Vihaan smiled, 'Don't worry about it. Sid knew a guy who worked backstage and is like the main coordinator of the event.'

'Thank you so much Vihaan!'

It warmed his heart to see Helen so happy and excited about something as simple as a theatre show. He realized how ungrateful he had been all his life for all the good things he had ever received or rather were provided for him by his parents. Somethings that meant almost nothing to him were a dream come true for others.

The show was a little early so they decided to head out for that before dinner. As exclusive as the tickets were, the theatre was tightly packed but Vihaan had managed to get Helen the best seats in the house. They took their places and as the lights were being dimmed Vihaan watched Helen as her eyes were starting to light up like lanterns in a dark night sky. Throughout the performance Helen explained the theme of the dance and showed him who the head choreographer was and talked about how The Enigma came into existence and what set them apart from the rest. Honestly Vihaan did not understand a single word she said as he was busy admiring her getting all excited, happy and talkative. He loved listening to her probably because up until now she had a very reserved attitude and didn't really open up to him. He still didn't know a lot about her as she often chose not to linger on the topic for too long, but they had all the time in the world to figure that out, he thought. This night was too perfect to be bothered about details like that.

It was around 8:30 pm when the show got over and Vihaan didn't feel like dropping her back home without offering her dinner first. 'Hey I'm a little hungry actually. If you don't mind maybe we can get some dinner before I drop you home.'

'Oh my god! I totally forgot about dinner. I am still reeling from that amazing show. But yeah, I guess I could eat something. Now that you've mentioned it, I'm hungry too.'

'Perfect, this new place has opened up somewhere in this block, got great reviews, but if you'd prefer somewhere else we can go there too.'

'Vihaan, you just gifted me an unforgettable evening of my life. I think I can trust you with dinner.'

Vihaan smiled and drove to the new restaurant that had opened up while Helen continued to talk about the show and asking him what were the things that he liked about it. They reached the restaurant and Helen asked Vihaan if he could place the order for her as well while excusing herself to use the ladies' room. The food came after a few minutes and since it was already late and both of them were really hungry, they were busy devouring the food. Needless to say, they finished up faster than any other table at the restaurant that night.

As Vihaan was paying the bill, Helen started coughing. It was a mild cough at first but then the frequency picked up quickly.

'Hey are you okay?'

'Yeah, I just need some water.'

Vihaan poured her some more water and she gulped it down quickly only to throw it back up immediately, only this time it was not water, there were splashes of blood on the pristine white tablecloth. People from the other tables around them were shocked and the restaurant got quiet for a second. Vihaan couldn't move his limbs fast enough. His mind was trying to process what was happening, there was a voice screaming in his head to help her and do something, but he felt frozen. It took him a moment to understand what was unfolding in front of him. Helen's face was starting to get purple and her throat was starting to swell. He pulled himself together and rushed to her side.

'Helen, talk to me what is happening?'

'My allergy....', said Helen in a barely audible raspy voice. She was struggling to breathe now.

'Come on I'm taking you to the hospital.'

As Vihaan tried helping her to her feet, Helen fell into his arms unconscious.

Still to this day Vihaan do not know how he managed to get her to the nearby hospital in 5 minutes but there was only one thing going on in his head like a mantra, he cannot lose her. Vihaan waited outside the Emergency Room as a doctor was examining her. After what seemed like ages, he was asked to go meet the Doctor.

'Hello doctor, is Helen alright? What happened?'

'Hello, please take a seat Mr. Vihaan.'

Vihaan walked inside and sat on one of the chairs in front of the doctor who took one last look at Helen's medical reports that had just been delivered to him.

'Mr. Vihaan, Helen was really lucky that you were there to help her tonight when this happened. Basically, it was an allergic reaction towards shellfish and seafood in general. It's called Anaphylaxis, a common allergic reaction among people, however, in Helen's case she's a little too sensitive to this. Its like what you might call a one in a million cases.'

'I... I don't understand doctor.'

'Usually someone with a seafood allergy experiences difficulty in breathing and swelling and that's about it but in Helen's case, this allergy is life threatening as in fatal. She absolutely cannot eat any type of seafood. If you were even a few minutes late to bringing her in, I'm afraid then we would've lost her.'

Vihaan took a long deep breath as he processed the new information the doctor had just disclosed. 'Doctor, can I see her?'

'Yes, she's resting, we got her a room because she needs to be in observation here tonight, and if no other symptoms show up by morning then you have the all clear to take her home.'

'Thank you Doctor.'

Vihaan dashed out the door to the room and he watched her sleeping on the hospital bed through the window right before he entered the room. Quiet as a cat so as to not wake her up, he opened the door and walked in, sat down next to her and watched her sleeping so peacefully, her chest moving up and down ever so slightly giving him the only indication and assurance that she's still alive. He took her hand in his, nothing from her side, the sedatives must be very strong, but it's okay she needs to rest, she's safe now.

A few hours passed and Helen opened her eyes, her vision a little blurry at first but as her eyes started adjusting to the light of the hospital room and her brain started processing what happened that night, and how she wound up in a hospital after going out for a date, her eyes landed on Vihaan. Sleeping in a rather uncomfortable looking position for his tall body on a tiny couch in the room. He looked exhausted and very cute drooling a little on the hand rest of the couch. She tried reaching for the glass of water nearby without waking him up but her body was so stiff by now that she let out a little groan of pain at the first movement after a deep slumber. Vihaan was immediately up like an alert dog at the sound of her and was looked glad and relieved to see her awake and sitting up. He noticed that she was reaching for the water and rushed towards her and brought the glass to her. She took a few sips and kept it aside and asked Vihaan to sit next to her.

'Why are you still here?' asked Helen, her voice tired.

'What do you mean? How could I leave you here in that state?'

'It's nothing, just a small allergy.'

'It's not nothing, Helen. I would've lost you. I should've been more careful when I ordered the food. This is all on me.'

'Hey hey... don't say that Vihaan', Helen took his hand in hers.

When she spoke again, she sounded like a different Helen, one who was feeling very grateful 'I should've checked the food before I ate it. You didn't know about my allergy. I was so excited after that show that I forgot about everything else. But thank you so much for helping me and .... And staying back even at this hour.'

'Don't thank me. When you were inside and the doctors asked me to wait, every minute out there I was thinking of the worst and I if anything happened to you then I wouldn't be able to forgive myself. Ever.'

Helen squeezed Vihaan's hand tightly and said, 'You know I have only been in a hospital overnight like this a couple of times before but back then I was all alone. This is the first time somebody stayed back for me.'

'Of course, I'd stay back for you Helen, I love you.'

Both of them paused for a brief moment as he said those words out loud.

Vihaan cleared his throat and said ,'I mean... I'm sorry, you should be resting up, please go back to sleep, I shouldn't have...'

'Vihaan.....'

'Yeah?'

'Would you mind lying down next to me, I think I can sleep better if you're by my side.'

Vihaan couldn't believe what he had just heard. Carefully as to not disturb any of the monitor wires and tubes that were attached to Helen, he climbed inside the bed with her. She moved closer and snuggled into his chest inhaling feebly. He held her close gently.

'Vihaan?'

'Yeah?'

'You're a really nice guy....'

Vihaan knew a friendzone was approaching when a girl started her sentence exactly like this. He mentally embraced himself for the inevitable and asked, 'But...?'

Helen took a deep breath and when she spoke, her voice was had a hidden pain beneath it, 'Love is a complicated and a really big step for me Vihaan. There are still a lot of things that you don't know about me and I'm afraid that when you do get to know those things you might look at me differently. I haven't been in a relationship in a very long time. I don't even go out on dates anymore but I had a different gut feeling about you. And I'm glad that I agreed to go out with you tonight. I don't have a lot of friends, I'm mostly on my own but I was never worried about anything. But tonight, at that restaurant, I thought that was the end for me, I didn't think that I'd open my eyes again. But then I did, and the first person I saw was you.' She paused for a second and then looked up to him and said, 'I really like you Vihaan, I have since the first night we met when you took me home from that party, but I am really scared to be in a relationship.'

In his mind Vihaan was cursing the asshole who had hurt her so badly in the past that she is so scared to give anyone a chance now and had decided to live out the rest of her life alone. How could someone torture a poor soul like Helen? He knew that this was probably the end of their story. It started and ended quickly but it was his absolute favorite story and he wished they could spend at least a few more hours together until the break of dawn. To his pleasant surprise, Helen spoke again, her voice more confident now. 'I couldn't bring myself to trust anyone after my last relationship, for the longest time. And then you appeared out of nowhere that night. And for some stupid reason, every time we go out, I end up falling sick. But you didn't leave my side then and you didn't leave me now. So, I guess what I'm trying to say is, I want to give this a shot, I want to give us a chance. But please understand that I am not yet where you are right now and it might take me a little while to get there but I really like you Vihaan and something tells me that I'd be a fool to let you go.'

Vihaan was consuming every word she had said. He knew she was only putting up the tough front because she was scared on the inside and he felt bad that she had to go through a bad phase like that with someone. But she won't be sad and afraid anymore. He won't let her. Vihaan pulled her chin up to make her face him and asked in a sweet voice, 'Helen, would you like to be my girlfriend.'

She looked into his eyes, smiled and said, 'Yes!'

He planted a soft kiss on her forehead and they both drifted into a deep sleep, exhausted but extremely happy to have found each other.

Chapter-13

Annie

The courthouse was crowded as usual but today Annie felt something special in the air. Maybe it was the taste of freedom that she could almost taste. The final verdict on her and Alex's divorce was coming out today. After months of waiting, losing Daisy to him, and going for those ridiculous sessions with Dr. Ahaana, today was the day she could finally break free from all of that. She regrets rambling so much about herself to Dr. Ahaana in one of their previous sessions. If she wants to escape this place and start fresh in a new place then anonymity has to be her best disguise which is why she went back to being quiet in the next two sessions. But that doctor was good, Annie thought. Maybe it was the fact that she played those woman cards accurately or maybe she actually felt Annie's pain and was simply empathetic towards her and wanted to help her. No. Annie forced herself to stop her train of thoughts right there. This is exactly what that doctor wanted her to think, it's like she's walking right into that trap. How could she be so gullible? Going forward she had to be smarter than this.

Annie was distracted from her thoughts by a familiar voice next to her.

'Hi Annie', it was her now almost ex-husband Alex.

'Hi Alex. What do you want?' responded Annie in a very uninterested tone.

'Annie, I know that maybe it's too late. But can we talk? Please?'

'Talk about what?'

'Can we re-think this please? Let me help you. We really don't need to do this.'

'I don't need your help. And maybe you should've thought about it before you kicked me out of our apartment that night.'

'But Annie I did not…'

He was cut short mid-sentence by their advocates calling out both of them to appear in front of the judge.

A few crucial minutes later Annie and Alex came out of the courthouse, one feeling extremely happy and the other looking defeated having lost the last straw of hope. He felt like he was drowning in a deep dark water of nothingness. He watched as Annie walked out of the court grounds not even turning back to give him one last glance.

Chapter-14

Ahaana

It's been four weeks now and a no show from Annie. Ahaana knew something was wrong. She thought she had a break through with her silent patient. Annie had endured a lot over the years, but if she did not have the right spaces to let out her long-suppressed anger and frustrations, the consequences could be deadly. This was a patient who looked meek and soft on the outside but who was capable of doing dangerous things if she lost control of herself. And from what Ahaana observed, Annie was at the tipping point already. What if something triggered her already? Ahaana once again checked Annie's patient file. She found an address under the name of Mrs. Rodriguez who was also named as Annie's legal guardian. This is totally out of character for Ahaana and probably completely unnecessary too but she decided to go to the address and find out what had happened.

Ahaana was standing in front of the building where Mrs. Rodriguez's house was supposed to be according to the address in the file. It was a fairly old building with an old 80's charm to it because they had retained some of the fixtures as it is and it was standing out from the rest of the sky high glossy new apartments that popped up in every corner of the city lately. Ahaana went inside and she couldn't ignore the strange feeling inside her gut that told her she was not going to like what she was about to find out.

She was in front of Mrs. Rodriguez's apartment. The name was right outside the door. Ahaana rang the doorbell. Once. Twice. No reply. She rand it a couple more times, still nothing. Somebody opened the door of their apartment behind Ahaana and she turned back to look at the neighbor.

'Hi, can I help you?' asked the neighbor, a short stout lady in her 50s who looked really displeased at this mild noise pollution that Ahaana has been stirring up in the last 15 minutes.

'Hello, I'm really sorry for disturbing you,' replied Ahaana judging from the lady's frown realizing that she's a little pissed off already, 'but I am looking for a Mrs. Rodriguez. Does she live here?'

'More like used to live here.'

'What do you mean? She moved to a new place now?'

'No. She passed away a month ago.'

'Oh…I'm sorry…' If Mrs. Rodriguez had passed away then where was Annie?

'Who are you again?' the lady asked.

'I'm Dr. Ahaana, I'm a psychiatrist and actually I'm here to see a woman named Annie. She mentioned that she lived here with Mrs. Rodriguez. Would you know anything about her?'

'Oh, that young girl. Yeah, she was a character. Wouldn't get out or talk to anyone here, just like Mrs. Rodriguez, no wonder they got along so well. But you are wasting your time at that door. Nobody lives there anymore.'

'Oh I see. Would you by any chance know where she went?'

'No. Just left the place a few days later. Didn't say anything to any of us.'

'You didn't find that weird?'

'Everything about that girl was weird since the day she moved in. Mrs. Rodriguez used to visit me occasionally, we would sit and chat over some tea. But ever since she moved in, that stopped gradually. I was looking forward to getting to know her but she wouldn't even let anybody into the apartment. Every time I tried to check up on Mrs. Rodriguez, Annie would say that she was either sleeping, or in the shower, or not feeling great. I gave up after sometime.'

'You didn't try calling her?'

'She had lost her phone it seems. She didn't give me the new number or anything.'

'When did that happen?'

'I don't know maybe a couple of months ago. Not sure.'

'When was the last time you saw Mrs. Rodriguez?'

'The morning when we found out that she was dead.' The lady took a deep breath and shuddered at the memory. 'I woke up to a loud banging on my door. It was almost 6 or 6:30 in the morning because I was just getting up. It was the young lady knocking at my door, she was crying a lot too. She was calling me for help. When I went over and checked I saw Mrs. Rodriguez in the bed, cold. I immediately called an ambulance but when they reached here they told me she'd already been dead for hours. Some us got together and arranged a funeral for her and that was it. Poor girl was crying so much during the whole thing.'

'You didn't feel anything unusual about hear death?'

'What do you mean unusual? The woman was over 80, had chronic asthma and could barely walk. I mean it was going to happen any day now.'

'So, are you saying that she passed away in her sleep?'

'Hey I'm not saying anything, that Annie girl is the one who told us that Mrs. Rodriguez went to bed early that night around 9:30 PM after an early dinner. Said she was fine at that time. And then she didn't wake up when Annie brought her morning tea.'

'I see. Did Mrs. Rodriguez have any relatives?'

'Mrs. Rodriguez? Oh no. Her daughter passed away in an accident when she was maybe 18 I think. She was a really good kid, poor thing. And maybe a year and a half after that Mr. Rodriguez passed away too.'

Ahaana suddenly felt a wave of sympathy for this woman that she'd never met. No wonder she took Annie in.

'You haven't heard anything again from Annie after that?'

'No. Wait, I did get this a few days after Mrs. Rodriguez passed away.'

The woman went inside and brought back a small note and gave it to Ahaana.

Hi Aunty,

Thank you for all the help with the funeral. With Mrs. Rodriguez gone, there's nothing left for me here or nobody. So, I'm leaving. Once again thank you for all the help.

Yours truly,

Annie

'Initially, I thought that she was just shy to talk to us but then after we helped her out at the funeral, I really thought that she might be more friendly and inviting towards us. But nothing. She left one fine morning. I seriously don't know what Mrs. Rodriguez even saw in her to write off everything in her will to this girl. Guess everything worked out well for Annie anyways.'

'Wait, what did you just say?'

'Oh yes, the day after the funeral, Mrs. Rodriguez's lawyer came over. I was there with Annie dropping off some food, you know. This lawyer came in and asked us who was Annie. And then he said that Mrs. Rodriguez had recently updated her will a few months back. Apparently, she had decent money. So initially all of that was supposed to go to some charity or a trust. He mentioned a name, I can't remember it. Then a few months after Annie moved in with her, she updated her will and all of her wealth went to Annie.'

'How did Annie react to that?'

'Nothing special I mean, she started crying again and said that she didn't take care of Mrs. Rodriguez for the money. That she was like a mother to her.'

'And she left soon after the lawyer's visit?'

'I think around 2 days after that.'

'Would you know the name of the lawyer.'

'No. Now if you're done I have some cooking left to do.'

Ahaana gave the note back to the lady, thanked her and left the building. Once she was in her car, she couldn't push away the feeling that something terrible had happened and Annie was trying to cover it up. There is definitely more to Annie and she was going to find out what actually happened.

Chapter-15

Vihaan

What was supposed to be a fun meetup and probably an emotional one had turned out to be super awkward between his sister and his girlfriend. Ahaana seemed fine and happy even, right before she met Helen. But ever since Helen joined them at the restaurant, it was as if he could cut through the tension in the air with a knife. He decided to get some food on the table hoping maybe that could be an ice breaker between them.

'Didi what would you like to have?'

'Oh… um anything really, I don't mind.'

'Why you don't like this place?'

'No, it's not that. You can order for me, since you're the foodie after all.' He noticed that even when she said this her focus seemed to be elsewhere. Her mood had shifted. He turned to Helen.

'Helen?'

'…'

'Babe?' he nudged her a little and she blinked and snapped out of whatever was occupying her thoughts.

'Babe you okay? Something on your mind?'

'No… sorry, it's just a headache.'

'What happened?', asked Vihaan.

'Just a little stressed about the upcoming program.'

'What program?' the question was posed by Ahaana this time. Vihaan was glad that finally his sister was taking some interest in his girlfriend.

'Didi Helen is a dancer and she owns a dance studio in JP Nagar. It's been gaining popularity lately and she just landed a big show in December. This international artist is coming to Bangalore for a concert and they wanted some really good performers onstage and guess who landed the job?' Vihaan looked at Helen proudly.

'Congratulations… Helen.' Vihaan noticed that there was a slight emphasis when she said Helen's name. Does she not approve of her? Was it because she's a dancer compared to them? He knew his sister was way better than that, discriminating somebody on the basis of their profession and social status. His parents might find this an issue, a successful entrepreneur dating a dancer, and that's exactly why he needs his sister's support to break this news to their parents. But going by the looks of how dull this meetup was, Vihaan had started losing hope on winning his sister's support.

The waiter was at the table taking their orders now and as he was repeating Helen's order he asked, 'Sir would you like to try our signature shrimp Ramen? It's our bestseller.'

'Oh no no. No seafood for us please. Actually, could you please make sure that none of the food have any fish or fish sauce or oils?'

'Sure Sir.'

'That'll be all Thank You.'

'You stopped eating fish now? You love fish Vihaan. You should get some for yourself.'

'Actually Didi, Helen is allergic to seafood and ever since then I don't eat seafood whenever we eat out.'

Ahaana's eyes shot up at Helen.

'What kind of allergy are we talking about? If you don't mind me asking?'

'It's Anaphylaxis.' Said Helen.

'Actually, Didi it was a funny story, well, not so funny when it happened but it all worked out well for us. We went out on our first proper date to a new restaurant and when she was at the washroom, I placed the order, and it had a fish curry among other things. Once we finished eating and was about to leave she started getting terribly sick and vomited. I knew something was wrong and took her to the hospital as fast as I could and that's when I found out about this allergy. I was so worried for her that night, it really was like a life and death situation. But we pulled through, didn't we?' Vihaan looked at Helen lovingly as he pulled her towards him. Helen smiled uncomfortably.

'I'm glad that you recovered, better be careful than regret later right?' said Ahaana eyeing Helen. Helen did not say anything back.

The lunch was eerily quiet. Vihaan really had hoped for more excitement between the ladies. But he couldn't figure out what was happening. Helen finished eating first and excused herself to use the washroom. As soon as she left the table Ahaana started speaking, 'Vihaan how long have you known Helen?'

'Around 2 years I would say. Why?'

'Vihaan, Helen is not who you think she is?'

Vihaan was startled at this remark. This was unexpected. Did his sister know her before? He stopped eating and asked Ahaana, 'What …. What do you mean Didi?'

'She is lying to you. Her name is not even Helen. She's Annie.'

'What are you saying? Listen, Didi if you did not like her just tell me that but please don't say things like this.'

'Vihaan you've known her for 2 years, right? I met her long before that. I cannot explain it right now but please you have to believe me. Come by my apartment tomorrow and I'll tell you everything.'

Vihaan looked at his sister. It was a serious accusation. He felt uneasy hearing his sister talk about his girlfriend this way and that too just when he was about to propose to Helen. Tonight. He thought for a moment and said, 'Okay I'll meet you tomorrow.'

'Thank you. And Vihaan please be extremely careful around her. She's a dangerous woman.'

Chapter - 16

Ahaana

Ahaana felt a throbbing pain in her head ever since she got back from the restaurant after meeting Vihaan and Helen, or rather, Annie. She's been going over the incidents in a loop and every time she gets stuck and overstresses on something, the headaches start hitting. Had it been work stress she wouldn't have been so confused, as she always tried to leave work at the office and come home to a peaceful evening. But this was about her brother's life, which was not safe in Annie's hands. Maybe if the police had investigated Mrs. Rodriguez's death that day, the investigation would have led to Annie, but nobody even thought of it. Nobody wanted it was a more accurate way to put it. Everybody wanted to carry on with their lives. There was no blood relative left for Mrs. Rodriguez and the neighbors in the apartment building thought that it was a natural death of an old lady. If she didn't know Annie as her patient probably even she wouldn't have thought so much into this.

Seven years back when she left Mrs. Rodriguez's apartment that day after talking to her neighbor, she remembered that it was her friend Rahul who pleaded her to take up this case in the first place. He had told her that Annie's husband Alex was a dear friend and that he didn't have a lot of acquaintances in the city to help him out. Ahaana was initially reluctant to take up the case mainly because her schedule was fully occupied and she couldn't spare any other slots. But something about the arrangement caught her attention. The husband, Alex was ready to pay for Annie's sessions even though they were separated at the moment and were headed for a divorce. This was in fact an 'informal' clause he additionally added if he had to willingly sign the divorce petition. Strange! If Ahaana could get hold of Alex, then she'll probably know more about Annie. She silently blamed herself for not doing this sooner. She dialed up Rahul.

'Hey Rahul, how are you?'

'Ahaana! Always a pleasure to hear from you. What's up?'

'I was wondering if you could get me the contact details of your friend, Mr. Alex. You referred his wife's case to me a few months ago. Remember? A woman named Annie.'

'Yeah I remember. Unfortunately, I don't think I can help you out.'

'What do you mean?'

'Well, the divorce went through and shortly after that Alex quit his job at the hospital and left the city.'

'Do you know where he went? Maybe an address?'

'Not really. But why are you asking me this now?'

'His wife, Annie has not turned up for the last 4 sessions and when I tried to follow up with her legal guardian, one Mrs. Rodriguez, well, I found out that she was dead a month ago. And no news of Annie after that. Looks like she left too.'

'Okay. That's something! Listen Ahaana, I don't think you should go after this. The wife Annie, she was a piece of work from what I've heard. This could turn out to be really dangerous for you Ahaana. Its not safe. Just forget about this whole thing.'

'Rahul, he was your friend. You brought this case to me.'

'I agree. And right now, I'm telling you to let this go. Please.'

Ahaana thought about it for a good long minute. Rahul was right, she is just finding her footing and this is not the right time to play Nancy Drew. Besides Annie is not her problem anymore. Nobody has any complaints about whatever went down in that apartment then why should she bother?

And that right there was a big mistake, thought Ahaana now. She should have pursued that case because her gut told her then and now that Annie had some involvement in Mrs. Rodriguez's death. It all happened way too conveniently for Annie. Nobody was that lucky. She should know that.

Ahaana sat down on her bed, opened the drawer of her nightstand and took a framed photo from inside. It was a picture of her and Zayyan on a beach. Sometimes when she missed him a lot she looks at this photo and talks to him. Zayyan had a very infectious smile. It was the kind that radiated so much warmth, more than even words could ever convey. In the picture, he is hugging her tightly, her eyes closed resting her head on his chest with a smile on her face, she cannot remember another time when she looked and felt so perfectly happy with someone. Zayyan resting his chin on top of her with a slight tilt of his head, had the look of a man who had the world with him. Both of them were so young and happy back then, dreaming of their whole lives ahead, a lifetime left to make endless memories together. But they didn't know that this was the last time they would be together, that this was going to be the last picture she will ever have of him, that evening was the last time she will ever see him alive. A tear drop fell on the photo on Zayyan's face. Ahaana slid down from the bed, onto the floor and let it all out. She hugged the picture close to her heart yearning to feel his embrace one more time, for him to pull her into a tight hug and whisper in her ear once more that everything will be okay, to feel his warmth and the sound of his beating heart against his chest one more time. 'Why did you leave Zayyan? Its so hard without you. I cannot do this anymore. I miss you so much!'

Not a lot of their classmates were aware of Ahaana and Zayyan's relationship. She was the daughter of one of the most renowned doctors in Mumbai, and people always love to stir up a scandal in what looks like a perfect, happy family on the outside. So, they'd sneak out every now and then whenever they could catch a break from classes and labs. Those three years with Zayyan were the only times when Ahaana loved herself. It was like she broke out of her shell and saw the world truly for what it was. And while it had an ugly side too, she understood that life did not come so easy to many as it had come to her. She learned so much from Zayyan and in a way he helped her evolve into a more caring and selfless individual.

It was one such evening when both of them had a few hours to spare before they went back home. Zayyan's sister Zeenath was getting engaged that evening and even though Ahaana said he should head home to help out his parents, he said he wanted to spend some time with her before that. So, they headed to the beach to watch the sunset together. They parked her car a little far away and walked towards the beach. They found a spot to sit but it was probably not the best day for a romantic beach getaway because the place was way too crowded. There were street vendors, kids playing football, a ton of tourists and they were lucky to even find a spot to sit even if that meant they were almost crammed between people.

'This is not really what I had in mind. There are way too many people here. I'm sorry', the disappointment couldn't be more evident in Zayyan's voice.

Ahaana laughed and said,' Don't worry, I have an idea.'

She reached inside her bag and took out her earphones and offered one earphone to him. He wore it on his left ear and she wore it on her right ear. The timing had just become perfect as the sun was starting to dip into the ocean, a flaming ball of red and orange, winking its final goodbye to the world. Ahaana played their favorite song. It was an old Bollywood song and the lyrics went like this,

'Embrace me for who knows if this beautiful night will ever be there again or not. For maybe in this lifetime we may or may not meet again.'

They looked at each other as the sun was setting. All the commotion around them seemed to be fading away in the background and it was just the two of them on that coast, two young souls deeply and unconditionally in love with each other and who were made for each other. Ahaana smiled a shy little smile at Zayyan. She clicked a picture of the two of them. After the sunset they headed back to the car and once they were inside, fastening her seatbelt she said, 'Whew!! that was a lot of people, I mean did you see....'

Before she could finish her sentence, she felt Zayyan pull her chin towards him, and the next thing she felt was his soft lips against hers and she melted against his kiss, gentle yet passionate, too overwhelmed to process what was even happening. There was an urge, a need and a thirst in that kiss, he was telling her how badly he wanted her at that moment. A warm sensation filled her body. She wanted him too so badly. Sometimes a gesture speaks more volumes than words, you can feel exactly what the other person is trying to tell you through a simple kiss. A moment later he pulled away and Ahaana opened her eyes, feeling stuck for words and waiting for them to come back to her.

'I'm sorry, I really wanted to kiss you since the moment you started playing that song, but there were too many people there. The beach is also close to your home and I was worried if somebody would see you with me.'

'Actually… um, I wished I could kiss you too.', was all Ahaana could manage to say. She was still trying to reeling out of that magnificent kiss.

'Wait are you blushing now? Aww you didn't expect me to do something so cheesy did you' asked Zayyan laughing at Ahaana, watching her as her cheeks turned rosy.

'No. shut up', she smiled and turned on the engine still trying hard to keep herself from blushing more.

Zayyan loved teasing her and he enjoyed watching her try to keep a straight face. They were pulling up in front of his house and she had just turned off the engine.

'Do you remember you asked me once what was the meaning behind my name?' asked Zayyan.

'Yeah I remember. But you had to be all mysterious and said you'll tell me when the time is right.'

'Okay I'll tell you now. 'Zayyan' means the one who makes things beautiful. But I don't agree because I feel like you make me a beautiful person.'

Ahaana laughed at Zayyan's yet another cheesy remark. And that's when he pulled out a small velvet box from inside his pocket and suddenly she stopped laughing, her eyes wide.

'Ahaana, I know that we still have a long way to go. And it might be too soon but no matter what happens I don't wanna lose you. You really make my world a better place and I love you for simply existing here. Ahaana Khanna will you marry me?'

He had opened the box now and inside was a simple ring with a tiny stone on top that looked like a diamond, she knew he couldn't afford a diamond but he must have been really saving up for this one and that too with his sister's engagement also happening at home. She looked at him and took his face in her hands and said, 'Zayyan, it's you or never. Yes'

He took the ring and put it on her finger. It fit perfectly on her small pale finger. She never took it off after that day.

After dropping Zayyan at his home, Ahaana reached her home to find her parents and Vihaan all sitting quietly in the living room. Her mother had a drink in her hand and Vihaan seemed very angry and upset for some reason.

'Hey what's going on? Why does everybody look so serious?'

Vihaan pushed her hand away when she touched his shoulder and went and sat next to him.

It was her father who spoke next, 'Who was that boy with you at the beach?'

'Wh… what do you mean Papa?'

Vihaan was furious when he spoke next,' I saw you kissing him in the car. How long has this been going on?'

Ahaana felt her whole body go cold and numb from her head to toe. This is definitely not how she had intended for her family to know about her and Zayyan. They would wait until Zayyan completed his PG and landed a good job at a multi-specialty hospital as a surgeon and by then Ahaana should be almost done with her final year too. Sure, religion was a big problem, family background was a bigger problem but both of them would be financially independent by then and she hoped that her father would understand her better then. This was happening way too soon and in the worst possible way. She wished she could just disappear.

'Tell me who is that boy Ahaana' demanded her father furiously.

'His name is Zayyan. And we love each other.'

'How long has this been going on?'

'3 years.'

'Are you out of your mind Didi?' Vihaan lashed out at his sister.

'Vihaan stop it. Ahaana listen to me. He is not the right guy for you. You are still too naïve to understand how these things work. When the time is right we'll find someone for you.' Said her father, trying to hold back his anger.

'So I don't have a say in my life?' Ahaana was starting to raise her voice now.

'You are too young to decide this' her mother spoke this time.

'I am an adult and this is my life Mumma. All this time I did everything like you guys wanted me to. I studied well, got good grades, never got into trouble. Always became the class topper. And all that time I never asked for anything in return. I don't even have any friends do you know that? Never did. Other kids saw me as a nerd and constantly made fun of me. The silent girl who never talks to anybody. I felt suffocated all that time, but I told myself this is what my parents wanted and I continued to slave away. When Zayyan came into my life that's when I felt what happiness is supposed to feel like. What living is supposed to feel like.' She was crying so now.

'So, your parents mean nothing to you?'

'That's not what I meant Papa.'

'No. I got what you meant. We have been making your life a living hell and he is the savior. We are the bad guys now, ' said her mother.

'Papa, Mumma, I want to do this with your blessing. You guys mean the world to me.' Pleaded Ahaana.

'If you mean it then leave him.' Demanded her father in a cold voice.

'No. I cannot do that.' Said Ahaana in a more stern voice.

'Think before you speak Ahaana.'

'Papa, please?' she asked in a soft pleading voice again.

'I'll give you two choices. Either you leave him, and we can all forget this day ever happened. You will go on to become a successful doctor like you were supposed to. But if you choose that boy over us, then you cannot live in this house anymore.'

Ahaana was shocked for a moment. Vihaan got up and her mother gasped. Ahaana became awfully quiet. She wiped her tears and went inside. Her father had a triumphant smile on his face. After all she was his daughter. He knew she'll only listen to her father. A few minutes later Ahaana came back with a duffel bag to everybody's dismay. She stopped in front of her parents and Vihaan and said, 'Just to be clear, I am the one who went after Zayyan. He never wished to put me in a spot where I'll have to choose between him and my family.' Ahaana's mother rose to protest against that statement but she raised her hand to stop her before she could say anything. 'Mumma please, hear me out. All this time I believed that my family would support me for anything I wanted and it has been like that ever since I could remember. But maybe I remembered things differently. Papa was always busy with his clinic and Mumma barely had any time for me and Vihaan. And I never complained. This is the first time I really went after something I loved and I would've never guessed that my family would make me choose. But since it has come to this anyway, I choose him.'

That was the last time Ahaana spoke to her parents as she walked out into the night, with her entire life packed in a bag.

She would've gone straight to Zayyan's house but then she remembered that it was his sister's engagement and the last thing she wanted was to drag him into her family drama. She decided that she'll let him know tomorrow. But she needed a place to crash for the night. Since she didn't have many friends in college, she decided to call Zayyan's best friend Rahul.

'Hello, Rahul, I need your help.'

'Hey Ahaana, sure what do you need?'

'I left my house. My brother caught me and Zayyan together at the beach earlier today and when I reached home I got into a huge fight with my family.'

'Oh my God! Wait so where are you now?'

'I am at a bus stop near my house and I need a place to stay tonight. I can move into a women's PG or hostel tomorrow. Please don't tell Zayyan by the way.'

'Too late for that I think, you're on speaker phone and Zayyan is next to me. We're at his house for Zeenath's engagement.'

Ahaana felt so stupid. Of course, his best friend would be at his sister's engagement. How did she not think of that? Zayyan wanted Ahaana to attend the ceremony too but she would have to spin a whole different web of lies to get out of the house this late. So, she had politely declined. Zayyan was the one who spoke now.

'Ahaana, why did you leave your house?'

'You don't know the things they were telling me. It was either this or lose you. And I cannot lose you. So, I left.'

'No Ahaana you shouldn't have done that. They're your parents, obviously they will be extremely protective of you. But this is not how you should have reacted. Anyways, don't worry we'll meet your parents tomorrow, together. I'll talk to them and we'll figure it out okay? Now wait there. I'm coming to pick you up, you're staying here tonight.'

'No I can't. Your relatives will be there. What will you tell them?'

'You let me worry about that.' Assured Zayyan but Ahaana did not want to create further problems in one more family tonight. So she refused again.

'Um... okay Rahul is suggesting that you can stay at his girlfriend Shilpa's place. Is that okay?'

'Yes, thank you so much guys.'

'Okay now stay there, I'll come pick you up in 20 mins.'

'Okay.'

'Hey, it's all going to be okay. I'm here for you, we'll sort this out together okay? I love you.'

'I love you too.'

And just like that Ahaana started waiting for Zayyan.

Zayyan borrowed Rahul's bike and left home. He did not like the idea of Ahaana waiting at that bus stop at this late hour. He needed to get to her as fast as he could. He was also thinking how was he going to patch this issue with her parents? He didn't have a lot to offer them at the moment. Guy from a middle-class family on his way to become a surgeon. His academic proficiency was all he had. The little savings that his family had was going towards his sister Zeenath's wedding. Once he started working, things would be much better. He would be able to provide for and take better care of Ahaana. But right now, as he was making it through the final stretch of his PG years, he was still just another broke student. He didn't check the speed of the bike which was now racing faster than his thoughts. He didn't see the blinding white lights of the truck coming towards him. And by the time he understood what it was, everything happened in a split second. He remembers the white light burning into his retinas, he remembers hearing a loud crash, he felt something jerk his body forward even when he tried holding on to the bike. Right before everything blacked out, in that last few seconds when he was lying on the tarmac, eyes half open, vision slightly blurry, watching the hot thick blood from his head pool in front of him, he felt stiff with shooting pains all over his body but even in that moment, before his eyes closed for one last time, all he could think of was Ahaana. He promised her that he will make things right and she was still waiting for him.

Chapter - 17

Vihaan

The apartment building was spacious and huge. His sister had really done well for herself. He walked into the building, it was still early in the morning but he barely slept the previous night. How could he after all those allegations that his sister made against his soon to be fiancé? He was at Ahaana's door now and rang the bell. The door opened and from the looks of it Ahaana also didn't sleep very well last night. He thought her eyes looked puffy. Was she crying all night?

'Hey I'm sorry to bother you so early in the morning', said Vihaan.

'That's okay. Come sit. I'll make you some coffee.'

'No, its okay Didi.'

Ahaana gave him a stern look that told him to stop being so formal.

'Or maybe I will have a coffee Didi.'

She sat down across him in her couch, over-looking the balcony, green tea for her and coffee for Vihaan. She took a sip and turned to face him and said, 'You must be thinking about what I told you at the restaurant last night.'

'Yes. That was a serious accusation you made against Helen. What was that about?'

'Vihaan before I tell you everything, I need you to keep an open mind.'

'Is this because I didn't support your relationship with Zayyan?' burst out Vihaan.

Ahaana was disappointed to hear this, 'What? How could you even think that Vihaan? I have taken care of you since you were a baby. I know you better than anyone and I would want nothing but happiness for you. Whether it's a partner or career, I only wish the best for you.'

Vihaan felt a little embarrassed jumping into conclusions about his sister a second ago.

'I'm sorry. But I need to know what's going on.'

'Her name is not Helen. Its Annie. At least, that's what she told me back then. It was around 7 seven years ago. I was working part-time in my own small clinic in Mumbai, a few months after I left home. It was my professor who suggested that I could start practicing after getting my license. My work was getting recognized faster than I thought. Soon, my clinic was running on full capacity and that's when my friend Rahul asked if I could take up one more client. I didn't want to at first but something about that case felt a little bit out of the ordinary.

'The patient's name was Annie, who was on the verge of divorce with her husband Alex but what got my attention was that it was her husband's clause in the divorce agreement that she should undergo treatment with a psychiatrist if he had to willingly sign the divorce petition. It was an informal clause, like an out of court settlement. It was not written there officially. Alex was the one paying for her sessions every time. I was getting my money so I didn't poke too much into it. Annie was an extremely silent patient. She didn't talk to me for the initial few sessions. Not a word. And then one day I got her to talk. She said a lot of things that day and had a lot of hatred towards her husband. But she adored her daughter, Daisy and would do anything to get her back from her husband's custody. But she again kept quiet for the next 2 sessions that followed and after that she stopped coming to see me altogether. Maybe she felt like she overshared with me. But 4 or 5 weeks went by and Annie was a no show. I tried contacting her but with no result. I pulled up the address she gave at the clinic and found out that she was living with an old lady in her 80's. Her name was Mrs. Rodriguez. But it was only when I went there in search of Annie, I heard from the neighbor that Mrs. Rodriguez died a month ago. Annie never interacted with anyone in that building and ever since she moved in, Mrs. Rodriguez also stopped meeting or talking to the neighbors. She made sure all sorts of communication was cut off and the only way you could reach out to someone was if you talked to them in person. Mrs. Rodriguez had no family and she had transferred all of her assets and money to Annie before she died. After that, nobody ever saw Annie. I tried contacting her husband through my friend Rahul who brought this case to me in the first place and he told me that Alex had left the job after the divorce and he had no other contact details about him. I really wanted to talk to Alex, something I should've done earlier. He said Alex doubted that Annie was making things up sometimes but he was not sure if this was a serious issue or if she was experiencing this due to stress. Alex really seemed to care about her and loved her too but she had a lot of pent up rage inside her. I wanted to know more but Rahul stopped me from digging further into it.'

Vihaan listened to Ahaana and he was silent for some time. When Ahaana spoke again, her voice was filled with concern for her little brother, 'Vihaan, I know how you must be feeling now. I shouldn't have dumped all of this on to you. And trust me I'm not happy about it either. But if my suspicions are right, then your girlfriend could be a murderer.'

Vihaan lost his temper at that, 'Oh would you please stop this nonsense please?'

Ahaana was taken aback. That was definitely not the reaction she was expecting from him. Vihaan continued trying hard to compose himself but his voice was giving him away.

'Okay, so Helen has a past alright? What's the big deal here? Don't I have one too?'

'But that's different.'

'How is it any different? And for your information, I knew that she was divorced and have a child. She told me all this a long time ago.'

'Are you serious? Then why would you want someone like this as your partner?'

'Wait, let me get this straight, so when you fell in love with Zayyan, it is justified but when I love someone who happened to be a divorcee and has a child, that's atrocious? You know what Didi, I thought even if nobody took my side, you out of all the people would understand me. And I thought you'd help me convince Mumma and Papa. But look at you accusing her of murder and all. This is like a bloody nightmare.'

'So you believe her word over mine now?'

'Yeah maybe I do. Because you were never around. You just left and never looked back.'

'And you think that was easy for me? You still had food, a place to sleep, you were still taken care of while I was out there starving for days because I had no money or work or literally anybody to help me out. And then I heard that the only man I ever fell in love with was dead, Vihaan.

DEAD!! Can you even imagine what that feels like? Do you even know how many side jobs I had to take up to get me through college? And you accuse me of turning my back on you guys when you did not have my back.'

Vihaan was quiet. He couldn't bear to look up at her. He realized how selfish he had been. She was right after all, he dived into his problems and his wedding plans right after meeting her. He didn't even spend some quality time with his sister before he introduced her to Helen.

'Didi I'm sorry. I really am. But I really love Helen. She told me how horribly her ex-husband used to treat her. She said if I wanted to leave her even after knowing all of that, I still could. I think that's pretty brave of her to say something like that to me, knowing that she could end up being alone the very next minute. Please try to understand. I don't know any better way to say this but she changed me into a better man. Why don't you try to listen to her side of the story for once?'

Ahaana turned and walked towards her open balcony, taking a deep breath hoping some fresh air might clear all the terrible feelings that's been churning up inside her. She turned to look at Vihaan and said, 'Fine. I'll give this a fair chance. I want to talk to her.'

Chapter-18

Annie

She reached out frantically for her pill bottle only to see that it was empty. As she started blaming her carelessness on how she forgot to refill her anxiety medication she realized that Ahaana was the root cause of all this. Her life was going even better than she had planned but this doctor had to be his goddamn sister out of all the other billion people in the world. Had it been anybody else, she could have just sweet talked her way into becoming their absolute favorite. It would be a win-win situation for everybody. But it won't be that easy to fool this doctor. And now she had asked to meet her. Alone. What was she planning?

Ahaana asked to meet Annie at her new clinic. Annie was not only feeling too great about the idea of meeting Ahaana alone but this was worse. She got the weird feeling that meeting at her clinic was part of some kind of a plan maybe. How difficult would it be for her to get a cup of coffee in literally any café in Bangalore? But Annie knew that she had to keep her feelings in check. She simply could not afford to make any mistakes now. As Annie approached the door of the clinic she realized that her anxiety had already started shooting up. She somehow had to get through this meeting. So, after taking a deep breath she walked inside.

The clinic was big and the décor was elegant and a little luxurious which was a stark contrast to the tiny, old, shabby clinic that Annie had first walked into 7 years ago. If that was a cramped two room space with hardly any furniture except for an old couch, a table and some chairs, this was an airy space, with pastel colored walls that radiated a heavenly feel with beautiful artworks, expensive furniture, light music in the background and some lush green plants making the clinic look more alive. It looks more like an expensive designer boutique or showroom and less like a place where people go to seek mental help. This is definitely not what Annie expected when she thought they were meeting at her 'clinic'. The place had a very positive and calming energy to it.

Ahaana came out to greet Annie. This is really the weirdest encounter that Annie's ever had. She ran away from this doctor years ago and now she is forced to go talk to her again. Does she know more than she's letting on? 'Hi, come in', said Ahaana. Annie followed her cue. 'Please take a seat Annie oops, sorry, Helen.' Annie had just pulled back a chair but this remark stopped her. She paused and looked at Ahaana contemplating whether to sit or leave here once and for all. But for how long is she going to run? She cannot give up Vihaan. He is her golden ticket after all. So, this is a little risk that comes with the opportunity and she needs to deal with it this time. She sat down.

'So, we meet again.' Ahaana opened the conversation.

'Yeah'

'I'm not going to lie. This is a really tough spot for me.'

'Tough spot for you? Yeah. Sure', thought Annie.

'I'm sorry I left the way I did last time.' Annie thought apologizing might be a good place to start.

'You think that's what I wanted to talk to you about?'

'I don't know.'

'Why do you think I wanted to see you Annie?'

'Please don't call me by that name' said Annie slightly getting irritated. This may not go well after all, she thought.

'Why? Because it reminds you of who you actually are?' asked Ahaana. Oh, so she is trying to break her, thought Annie.

'I've been nothing but honest to Vihaan.'

'You know nothing about Vihaan. Not the way I do. And please don't even start with honesty. I think we both know what the right thing is to do here. You need to leave him.'

'No. I love him.' Asserted Annie.

'Love? Seriously? I know what you're playing at. Last time I stayed out of your business but this time its personal for me. Leave Vihaan.'

Fine if this is how she wants to play it, she left her no choice.

'Doctor I don't need you to tell me what to do with my life.'

'Sure. Since you've already done more than enough. Like, you did with Mrs. Rodriguez or that poor ex-husband of yours.'

'What are you talking about?' it is getting difficult to maintain her calm demeanor with every passing second, but she needs to be in control.

'So, you're saying that the lady who gave you a home when you had nowhere else to go, just happened to make a will transferring all of her assets to you very conveniently right before she died and just in time when your divorce was also coming through?'

It's starting to happen. She can already feel the pain pulsing through her veins on her head. Annie is regretting agreeing to do this.

'Do you even realize what will happen when Vihaan finds out about this? He will hand you over to the cops himself. But I'm giving you an option to avoid all that drama and get out. Just like you did last time. If money is what you need then I can arrange it for you. But I want you out of my brother's life.'

'And what proof do you have?' The animal is out and there's no going back.

It was Ahaana who was quiet now.

'Yeah I thought so too. In fact, I think you already talked to Vihaan but looks like your baby brother did not believe anything you said. If you had any solid evidence you wouldn't be trying to bribe me to leave Vihaan. You would have handed me over to the cops yourself. All you have are words. Hollow, empty, words.'

'Annie I'm warning you. Don't go forward with this.'

'What do you think Vihaan would say if he heard you threatening me?' Annie was holding up her phone now, a satisfied smile playing on her lips, showing Ahaana that she had been recording their conversations all this time. She watched as Ahaana's face turned pale. She hit the stop button and said, 'Unless you want to lose your brother for another, lets say, 10-15 more years, you need to shut up and let him go through with this wedding. He is going to move back to America soon after the wedding and I will be out of your hair forever. You should be thanking me actually you know that? It was my idea asking him to patch things up with you.'

'Annie please don't hurt him. I'm begging you.' She was in tears now.

'Why would I hurt him doctor? After all he is my only chance to escape this shithole. But if anybody were to come in between us. Well that would be a different story.'

There was a knock at the door and Ahaana's assistant opened the door to remind her that her next patient was waiting.

'Oh, looks like you have a busy day ahead. I'll leave you to it doctor, oops I mean, sister-in-law.'

Chapter-19

Ahaana

It's the third consecutive night that Ahaana is lying on her bed sleepless, exhausted and staring at the blank ceiling. She faced hardships before, even reaching to this point in her life came with its fair share of misery and hard work. She has the luxury of living in her own house, that she bought with her own hard-earned money, she gets to go to places in her own car. While this is the kind of success that most people of her age crave and aspire to achieve, most of them are already in possession of certain quiet luxuries which they are completely unaware of and sometimes even ungrateful about. Most people come from a loving and stable family, where they are supported by parents and surrounded by their friends and siblings. You always have that person to seek advice from, to dump your boyfriend drama on, to complain about that nasty co-worker, to cheer you up whenever you feel low. Everybody had someone. But that's something Ahaana did not have in the last 7 years. She tied her love and dreams to one person, the only person she was comfortable with but fate wanted to burst that balloon for her. So, yes, she's successful but at the cost of these quiet luxuries in life. But now, life is giving her one more chance, to seek the love of her parents and her brother. Just imagining being able to walk into the house she grew up in and seeing her parents and hugging them, just a momentary thought of something so simple made Ahaana crave it more than anything else. But if she kept quiet, Vihaan's life will be in danger. Once Annie moves to America with Vihaan and realizes that her life is sorted, what will stop her from killing him to inherit his wealth?

Her phone rang in the tranquil silence of the room jerking Ahaana back from drowning further into her thoughts. It was Vihaan.

'Hi Vihaan what happened?'

'Hi Didi, so I have some good news. First of all I'm so thankful to you and really glad that you and Helen patched things up.'

Excuse me? Patched what up? That bitch! She's spinning this story to her advantage now. Ahaana was about to retaliate but stopped remembering the recording on Helen's phone.

'Hmmm.. but why are you calling so late? All okay?'

'Haha don't worry Didi. I wanted to ask you how quickly can you pack a bag and come with me?'

'What? I don't understand.'

'So, I was talking to Mumma and Papa and I told them about me and Helen', of course you did, thought Ahaana. 'And they were so happy for me. But they were even more excited when I told them that I reached out to you.'

'Wait, what did you tell them?' Ahaana was sitting up on her bed now, her heart pumping hard with anticipation of her parent's reaction. Was this a coincidence? She was just thinking about her parents a second ago.

'I told them that I reached out to you and that we've met a few times and before I could say anything more, Papa took the phone and asked all 3 of us to come over to our farmhouse in Pune. They are super excited to meet you Didi.'

'Oh my god!! I don't believe it!'

'Don't overthink it now. It's time to come home.'

As Ahaana cut the call she was overwhelmed with joy. Suddenly life seemed to be working in her favor. Finally, her parents accepted her for who she is. But like a dark cloud shading a perfectly blue sky, thoughts of Annie were seriously troubling her now.

Ahaana picked up her phone and called someone, 'Hi I really need your help and I cannot take No for an answer.'

The next day Vihaan came over for breakfast with his sister and they started making travel plans to leave for

Pune as soon as possible. Ahaana was in a good mood too. She had made Vihaan's favorite breakfast, poori and bhaji, set out a table in her balcony enjoying the pleasant Bangalore weather with their breakfast. She was catching up with his work too trying to figure out when would be a good weekend to go home.

'So, when exactly do you have the meeting with this American company?'

'On Saturday.'

'Can't you do it online?'

'Trust me, I wish I could but they're coming here to talk about a huge deal. I might have to move back to America for a few years if this deal goes through. I'll have to open a new office there and work closely with them to develop this new software. If we bag this, it'll put my company on the map. We'll be entering the big leagues.'

So that's what Annie was talking about that day. 'I see, are you nervous about it?'

'Honestly a little bit, I'm confident about my team. But I'm just afraid if I will be able to handle such a huge responsibility? Everybody will be counting on me.'

'Hey, you built this company on your own. Did everyone you came across back then say yes to every idea you had?'

'No'

'Did people run to help you out during your financial crises?'

'Hell No.'

'For most people, they'll drop their dream right there. But did you?'

'No.'

'So what did you do?'

'I tried finding a solution. I just didn't feel like giving up. I love this company so damn much.'

Ahaana loved watching her little brother talk so passionately about his brainchild.

'Remember Vihaan, something or the other will always obstruct your path. It could either be people or money or sometimes just situations. But you won't know what you're capable of until you go ahead and give it a shot.'

Vihaan looked at his sister and smiled.

'You really went through a lot didn't you.'

Ahaana didn't expect that for a reply.

'Um… yeah its nothing.'

'I really wish I was there for you.'

'You were a kid Vihaan. Any brother in your position would have done the same only. But look at me now. Maybe if things didn't happen the way it did, we wouldn't be here.'

'You do have a point there.'

'So... okay, this is an awkward question but are you seeing anyone now?' asked Vihaan a little carefully.

Ahaana almost spit on her green tea when she heard her brother's question. She started laughing. 'What? I barely have time to cook for myself and you think I'm on one of those apps swiping left and right?'

'No, that's not what I meant but you know... these things just happen. I just wanted you to know that, It would make me happy to know that you have someone in your life too. We all need a companion don't you think?'

'You make a good point but Vihaan, but I'm over that phase I think. Some love happens only once. And no matter how hard you try to forget it or replace them with someone new, it just doesn't feel the same way, you know. And why would I drag someone into my life now when I'm not fully in that mind space to give my all to them?'

'Do you miss him?'

Ahaana took a deep breath, put her teacup down and said without looking up, 'Every single day.'

'But,' continued Ahaana looking up now, 'unrequited love has a beauty of its own. When your worst fear just came true, nothing really shakes you anymore. You find a hidden inner strength that's bigger than yourself. I still feel that he's here with me. Guiding me through difficult times. Sure, I can't see or hear him. But he's there with me, as a part of me. I don't think that I can ever forget Zayyan. Our love has only grown deeper over time.'

There was silence for a moment. Ahaana thought she saw a new pain in her brother's eyes. Was it pain or guilt? But her phone started ringing and both of them were distracted from their moment. Ahaana answered the phone.

'Hello. I'll talk to you in some time is that okay? Yes. Thank you.'

'Who was that?'

'Um… that…. Well, looks like I have a conference to attend to next week. I don't think I can travel with you.'

'No but you said we'll go together.'

'I know, I'm really sorry Vihaan, but its kind of important. Won't take more than 3 days. I'll try to wrap things up as fast as I can and come home.'

'I guess we took after Papa since we're both such raging workaholics.'

'Yeah we sure did'

As Vihaan smiled and went back to devouring his poori, Ahaana watched him with concern in her eyes.

Chapter - 20

Vihaan

The plan was to finish the meeting as soon as he could and leave for Pune immediately. It was Saturday already and he couldn't believe how quickly this week flew by. It only felt like yesterday when he was having breakfast with his sister. It is a little unfortunate that she couldn't travel with him and Helen and he wondered if the conference she mentioned that day was something she made up simply because she wanted to avoid facing Helen after all the accusations she made about her. But he didn't like to think of his sister that way. It'll all be fine once they reach home, he thought.

Vihaan loved long drives and as much as people perceived him as this young dashing entrepreneur who was into partying and girls, he was the exact opposite now. Sure, he had a taste of that life before, when he was much younger and abroad but that Vihaan is a long lost memory to him now, like a figment of his imagination. He looked over to see Helen fast asleep on the passenger seat right next to him, her head on his shoulder as he drove. How could someone be this perfect even while sleeping he thought. It must be about 5 hours since they left Bangalore. There's 10 more hours of drive left. The expressway was pretty empty and the fact that it was almost midnight helped too. Maybe it was a little crazy of him to think that a long drive would be good. But he needed his brain to detach and unwind from work and the best way he knew to do that was with a long drive. He looked over again at Helen and thought back to the first time he drove her home. How she got car sick so bad. But look at her now fast asleep. They've been on a lot of long drives over the last 2 years, all of them duly planned and initiated by Helen because she knew what a thrill he got from driving so much and she wanted to get accustomed to his hobbies and likes. He couldn't even imagine that someone would do things like this, things that made them actually sick, just to make their loved one happy. He had a gem of a girl with him and he made a promise to himself that he's going to give her a lifetime full of happiness.

As if she heard him think about her so loudly, she woke up from her sleep.

'Hey sleepyhead' said Vihaan teasingly.

'Hey baby.'

'You alright there? Need a bathroom break?'

'No. I'm good. Would you like me to drive for some time?'

'No, you go back to sleep.'

'Are you sure? It been like 10 hours since we left right?'

He smiled and said, 'No baby its only 5 hours now. Don't worry about it. Come on go back to sleep.' Helen knew there was no fighting him when it came to who took the wheel. So, she happily gave up.

'Fine if u insist so badly.'

Chapter- 21

Annie

These next few days in Pune would be the final verdict on her acceptance into Vihaan's family. She had to be on her best behavior and if that meant acting like the perfect daughter-in-law to impress his parents then so be it. When she 'accidentally' bumped into Vihaan, she really did not think that things would reach at this point. Not that she didn't want to of course. She always knew that she wanted to move to America and live out the rest of her life there. But she didn't stand a very good chance of making that happen all by herself. It would seriously take a long time and she's been very lucky that nobody had bothered to look into her past for the last seven years. But she couldn't count on her luck alone. It was so much safer to leave the country and the best way to do that was by meeting someone rich and influential who wanted to settle down there. Ever since she moved to Bangalore, she's been slowly attempting to do that. She had dated a few men already but they were of no use.

When she first came to Bangalore she realized that she needed to re-invent herself, focus on a little grooming up to make sure she was attractive enough to catch the eye of a gentleman. She had the alimony from her divorce and a slightly bigger amount which she inherited from Mrs. Rodriguez. That was more than enough for her to live a comfortable life, for now. But it won't sustain her for very long. She applied for a few jobs in the initial days but then she was worried that these companies might do a background check on her and besides the more people she interacted with the easier it would be for the cops to track her down. But she needed to work for a living and that's when the idea of starting a dance studio popped in her head. That way, she could make just enough money to get by without touching this huge sum that she inherited until she found a way to move to a safer place. She did however, spent some of the money on finding a small dance studio, and giving herself a little makeover. She had a pretty face but she looked much older than she actually was thanks all those years of trauma. A little tweak here and there with some Botox and facelift would help make herself look younger again. Young and sophisticated. She did not want to be a mistress to a sleazy old man. That much she was sure of. Mistresses can always be replaced, but it's the wife who held all the power.

So, she found out who were some of the top rich people in the city and started attending their parties and events in the hope of being spotted. Sometimes it worked but most of the times it didn't. Even when somebody noticed her, they only wanted a one-night stand from her. She couldn't believe how many of these men, married men with wives and kids who looked so decent on the outside approached her with this intention. She would politely decline and move on to the next man every time that happened. But some other times escaping was not that easy. Slowly she realized that she was aiming at the wrong target market. She needed to approach someone more realistic, more practical and probably younger too. They might not be this wealthy but definitely wealthy enough to lead a comfortable life and take good care of her and Daisy. But the problem with 30-year olds was that they did not want to settle down that easy. Especially not when they were in a city like Bangalore. Some of them were not even ready to admit her as a girlfriend, since it's the season of situationships anyway. Seven years went by with futile attempts to find a right target and she finally decided to give up. She made it so long without getting caught. Maybe she might be lucky in the future too. It just meant that she'll have to wait a little longer until she could meet her daughter again.

Natasha was a student in Annie's dance class and she was the only one who was closer to her age among her students and for some reason she always felt good talking to Natasha. After so many years of living on your own and doing things on your own, it felt nice to have a girlfriend to go out and do things with. Natasha started talking about her boss Vihaan. How dashing and smart he was, how so different and driven he was from the others. That's when the idea struck Annie. A few months later Natasha was telling her that there was an office party and she wanted to go shopping for a dress with Annie. This was her chance. She asked if it would be possible for her to get invited into this party. Natasha was a little skeptical at first but Annie knew how to play with Natasha's weakness. She always felt very sympathetic towards Annie, whenever she talked about how lonely she felt in the big city. Finally, she got Natasha to agree to take her as the plus one. Now all she needed to do was meet Vihaan in the most coincidental way.

To Annie's surprise she noticed that this guy, unlike the other guys she'd met over time was really into her from the very beginning. He had easily levelled up the playing field for her now. But wait, men don't like a woman who threw herself on him. They loved to chase their woman. The more uninterested she pretended to be, the more desirable she seemed. So, on the night of that office party when Vihaan tried talking to her, she improvised and acted pissed off and irritated by his presence. It was like giving him a taste of what he could have and then snatching it away. Once the party was over, she stayed back to see if her bait worked. All she had to do was act like a damsel in distress, get Natasha drunk and send her off with Sid and turn off her phone and let Vihaan be her savior. But when she got car sick, which was not part of the plan, she thought her plan had backfired but he took really good care of her and still asked her out on an official date. That's when she was slightly confused. Her curiosity got the best of her when she ate the dish that contained fish knowing very well that it will trigger her allergic reaction. If she was going to be his wife in the future and if he was going to take care of her little girl, she had to make sure that this man was being true to his words. She assumed he might take her to the hospital but was astonished to see that he spent the whole night right next to her bed waiting for her to wake up. That was the moment when it stopped being an experiment for Annie. She knew that there was no way she will come across another guy like Vihaan. He was her escape and no matter what happened she had to marry him and leave the country.

Ahaana was the only problem in front of her now but even that threat looked minimal, now that she had something to blackmail her and keep her away from them just long enough. She snuggled up closer to Vihaan falling into a deep sleep knowing that this vacation was the beginning of the end. End of this cat and mouse game once and for all. She will be reunited with her darling daughter pretty soon and nothing can come in between them.

Chapter - 22

Ahaana

Guilty doesn't even begin to describe what Ahaana was feeling. Vihaan would lose his mind if he knew that his sister was still on his girlfriend's tail. Probably to the extent where he might regret reconnecting with his sister in the first place. But she can only hope that he will understand everything she did once he realizes that it was all for his own good. Ahaana was already in Mumbai a few days before Vihaan and Annie arrived in Pune. She wanted to know more about Annie and the one person who could help her out was her friend Rahul who first brought her case to Ahaana. Rahul was Zayyan's best friend and now a really close friend of Ahaana. His family owned and operated the RK Hospital franchise all over the city. When Rahul entered the family business he was in charge of working at one their busiest hospitals in the city which is where he met Alex who worked in the accounting department of the hospital.

'You need to tell me everything you know about Alex and Annie.' Ahaana asked Rahul after he agreed to help her out since she left him no choice. They met at a café near his hospital and she dived right into the issue at hand because she had been getting a strange gut feeling that every second counted now.

'Okay fine. As you know after I got my medical license, my father wanted me to look after the operations of this hospital. But he suggested that I lay low at least for the first couple of months so that the staff won't know who I am and I'll know how the place actually operates. It was during those months that I met Alex. To him I was just another new doctor working there for the monthly paycheck. Also, we were the only two young staff. The other doctors were more senior to us. But there was something different about Alex. I always felt that he had so little but he was always looking at the brighter side of things. Such a positive guy. He came to this city with his wife Annie, they had lots of dreams and were just starting a new life together. But things changed pretty soon. Annie wanted to own a dance studio to teach dance but Alex was trying to save up for a house, because Annie was not very happy with their current living situation. And that's when she found out she was pregnant and things really became difficult for him after that. He started keeping to himself, was working here overtime, to the extent where I called him up one day and asked him what was going on. He said things were not so great at home. He didn't elaborate on that and I didn't feel like asking more because it really felt like a private matter and I was his boss after all. He might not be comfortable sharing it with me. Few more weeks passed by and Alex seemed to become worse. I talked to him again and he said that his wife had filed for divorce but he felt like she was not her usual self. Now this fact, he was not completely sure of. He said there were noticeable behavioral changes and I suggested that maybe he could convince her somehow to go seek professional help. So, he made an unofficial clause in the divorce agreement where told her that he would willingly sign the papers only if she went to see a psychiatrist. But since the treatment was expensive and since I put him in that spot I decided to help him out. And that's where you came in.'

'Wow! Okay. I have never heard of anything like this before' exclaimed Ahaana.

'Yeah me too. Annie started coming to you but even then, Alex didn't seem to get better. And he started distancing himself from everyone.'

'And then the divorce went through?'

'Yes. Alex was a mess. I felt bad for the guy and took him out for a drink. He refused to have any. I tried talking to him about an upcoming promotion for him at work. He disrupted me saying that he wanted to see Annie.'

'Wait what? Is that the same night when Mrs. Rodriguez died?'

Rahul was quiet now. he seemed to be searching for the right words to speak to calm her down.

'Rahul tell me exactly what happened that night? Did Alex go over to Mrs. Rodriguez's house?'

'Yes. Eventually.'

'What do you mean?'

'When he said he wanted to meet her I told him it was a bad idea. But he was very stubborn about it and finally I told him that he should try calling her first.'

'If they talked then why did he go over there?'

'That's the part. He said that he called but Mrs. Rodriguez picked up the call. I didn't hear what he told her because the music was loud and he went outside the pub to talk to her. But when he came back he looked extremely distressed and said that he needed to go there immediately or something bad might happen.'

'Wait what time was it when he called Mrs. Rodriguez?'

'Around 11:00 pm. I remember because soon after the call he said that the pub was closing for the night and he booked me an Uber to get me home. I had a major surgery to attend the next morning so he made sure that I got home in time.'

'That is strange.'

'What is?'

'When I was at Mrs. Rodriguez's apartment a month after her death, looking for whereabouts of Annie, I talked to their neighbor who told me that Mrs. Rodriguez went to bed at 9:30 that night. That's what Annie told everyone in the building the next day.'

'Alex's phone was on speaker when he called Annie and I heard an old lady's voice too when the call was picked up. In fact, the only reason he went outside to talk was because the lady had difficulty hearing him over the music.'

'What happened after he went there', Ahaana's heart was racing now thinking that this big mystery was finally coming to an end.

'Yeah so here's the thing. I didn't see him after that night.'

'What?'

'Yeah. He did not come to work the following morning or even for the next few days after that. I couldn't reach him over call. And when it was almost a week of him not showing up at work, I received an email from him saying that due to some family problems back home in Jaipur, he needed to move back there. He quit his job at the hospital. Honestly Ahaana, at that point I swear I had this creepy feeling that something shady was going on. I didn't want to be caught in between this mess. That's why I didn't tell you these things before.'

'It's okay I understand. You're a good friend Rahul. I just need one more favor from you.'

'What do you need?'

'We're going to meet Alex.'

Chapter - 23

Sometime in 2007

It was the annual Holi celebration in town. She wandered through the crowd in search of him. His name was Jay and bullies like him only walked around in packs, because they were cowards without their minions. But today she needed to get him alone. Fortunately, she wouldn't need anything to cover her face because everybody was drenched in colors and were running around like a bunch of chameleons in red, yellow and green. Her own parents won't be able to recognize her face underneath the explosion of colors on her face. And that's when she spotted him. A bunch of teenage boys similar to her age, throwing balloons filled with colored water on people passing by. He was easy to spot as he was the tallest one in the group. He was their school's pride. Everybody said that he had the potential to become a national or possibly even an international athlete. But that doesn't give him the license to be an asshole to others. She took it upon herself to teach him a little humility.

She walked towards the group of young boys and said, 'Hi, Jay, can I talk to you for a second?'. The other boys started howling and hooting and started hyping up their macho leader. 'Typical idiots', she thought. Jay approached her and asked her, 'Hey do I know you?', perfect, she thought. The fool doesn't recognize her! 'Listen, I wanted to give you something.' She said in a flirty voice. 'Yeah sure, what is it?' he asked and she could sense the eagerness in his voice. Boys this age are so stupid she thought. 'Um... I can't give it to you here, not in front of your friends. It has to be in private you know. Why don't you meet me behind that abandoned house at the end of the street in 10 minutes? And come alone.' She said moving closer to him now. She could practically hear his heart beat in her ears and the thirst in his eyes couldn't be more obvious. If there is one thing she knew about teenage boys, it was that they were extremely horny all the time. Give them a whiff of what they could have and they will listen to your every command. Especially the ones who loved to pretend like they were the alpha in a group, they turned out to be the easiest ones to toy with. She smiled at him and walked away.

10 minutes later she watched as he was walking towards the abandoned house. She was hiding behind the trees. He was behind the house now exactly where she wanted him and was excitedly waiting for this mystery girl. This was her moment. She took the firecrackers from a small cover in her hand. These were the kind that would blast like a bomb but the explosion would be small and controlled. It was still lethal and extremely dangerous if thrown at someone. And that's exactly what she did. She started lighting them up one by one and threw it at him. The first one fell at his feet.

People ran towards the noise of firecrackers but to their surprise it was followed by the cry of a young boy. Once they reached the scene they were shocked to see what happened. There was a teenage boy of about eighteen lying unconscious on the ground, with a lot of burns on his body, especially his legs. The boy was bleeding severely and his skin had peeled off on so many places. Someone called an ambulance and he was taken to the hospital. Once the crowd dispersed and the place was empty, she came out of hiding and observed the scene where she attacked him. She enjoyed watching him scream out in pain as he fell to the ground and she still continued to throw more firecrackers at him. She simply did not stop. And as she was about to walk back she noticed a small chunk of one of his shoes with his name 'Jay' engraved on it. She took it with her.

A few days later, during the morning assembly, the principal announced to the whole school that their star athlete Jay had to undergo a surgery as he was involved in an unfortunate accident during Holi. He wouldn't be able to play for their school football team that year. In fact, he might not be able to play for a very long time. Many gasps could be heard among the students and even teachers. But one girl among the students smiled, an evil, wicked smile.

Chapter - 24

Vihaan

It was still quite early in the morning when Vihaan and Helen arrived at his farmhouse. He didn't want to reach too early in case they might disturb his parents. 6:30 seemed like a good time. His father was already out jogging making the best out of the fresh air in the countryside. He always thought that his father was born to join the military, because the man's discipline is impeccable. His mother on the other hand was probably asleep. His parents made a very strange couple, now that he thought about it. His father was man who took a lot of pride in his work, health and punctuality. He was a man with a plan. It could be a normal Tuesday, but he would have a detailed idea about his routine and where he will be and what exactly he would be doing at any given point that day. This was something that his sister also inherited from their father. He always thought that they got along better than he ever could. Then there was his mother. She never took anything too seriously and definitely did not have a plan about almost anything. She enjoyed her social connections and being an exemplary host to her kitty parties and exhibitions, but he had to agree, she really was an exceptional host and really made up for all the other times when she lounged around with a glass of wine instead of focusing on being an active mother to her children. She had a great eye for art and all the finer things in life and while some might call it materialistic, he liked to think that she had exquisite taste. She was a good mother now, or she tried to at least. But her drinking habit really got the best of her during Vihaan and Ahaana's childhood. His father would be busy with his work and his mother was always out at one of her parties and both of them really did ignore their children. His mother gave up drinking and has been sober ever since he was caught using drugs after Ahaana left home. A huge fight broke out between his parents and his father blamed his mother for setting such a bad example for their son. That really struck a chord with her and he never saw her drink ever again.

To him, his sister was more of a motherly figure during his early years. His parents also fought a lot and every time an argument broke out little Vihaan ran to his sister. She always knew the right thing to say and she said it so calmly and put him to sleep. Now when he thought back to it he realized how scared she too must have been but she always protected her little one. He cannot remember seeing Ahaana scared about anything ever.

Vihaan and Helen got out of the car just as his father was completing his final lap around the grounds. His mother came out to greet them too. He had mentioned to his parents about Helen as his girlfriend and that they were getting serious about each other. Probably because the parents still feels bad about losing their daughter once, they did not reject him altogether, but they were not exactly overjoyed about it. Vihaan went and hugged his father and his mother and Helen also went and touched their feet as the culturally appropriate way to seek blessings from elders before hugging his mother. He noticed that both of them were still looking at the car as if waiting to see someone else step out of it and mildly ignored Helen. He realized that all this excitement was to see his sister. So he smiled and said, 'Sorry guys, Didi was not able to make it here with us.'

'What do you mean she…. She's not coming home?' his father's face fell as he asked his question and he noticed that his mother's smile also faded and a slight concern creased her forehead.

'No, she will reach here tonight. She had to attend a conference last minute. So, she couldn't travel with me and Helen. I promised you guys that I'll bring your favorite child home, right? If I said it, you know I'll make it happen.'

'Oh, come on we don't have favorites.' Said his mother a little embarrassed.

'Yeah right, you don't' teased Vihaan as they all went inside the house.

The farmhouse was lovely, a stark contrast to the bustling city with its noise and people. There was a lot of quiet and vast stretches of land here with a lush green scenery. The air also felt cleaner and Vihaan knew that it was a great idea to bring everybody together here. As a child, some of his happiest moments with his family happened here. If he was being honest, he was a little worried whether his father might still be angry at her, but after knowing that they've been waiting impatiently for her, he was relieved. He went to Helen's room and saw that she was standing by the window lost in thoughts. He walked up to her silently and hugged her from behind.

'Hey beautiful. What are you think about?'

'Hey! Oh …. Nothing. It's really silent here and I think that'll take some getting used to.'

'Yeah it is very silent here. But in a nice way, right?'

'Sure. Any news about when your sister will reach here?'

'Yeah actually I was just talking to her and she should be getting here by late evening. I can't wait for that moment. It's been 10 years since Mumma and Papa saw her. And this is all thanks to you.'

'What did I do?'

'If I hadn't met you I probably wouldn't have reached out to my sister even now.'

'Oh right. Yeah.'

'Hey you okay? You seem a little pale. Are you sick?'

'No, just a little tired. It was a long journey.'

'Yes, and my brave little soldier did not throw up this time. Bravo!' teased Vihaan

'You better leave now or I might throw up on you right now.' chuckled Helen playfully pushing him away.

'Okay okay I'll leave and let you rest for some time before my sister gets here.'

'Thank you. I'll see you in the evening.'

Chapter - 25

Annie

You could be the perfect girlfriend, or an amazing wife or even the perfect mother but you can never replace a daughter in a family, no matter how hard you try. When she saw how eager and excited Vihaan's parents were to meet their daughter, Annie was a little sad. She never received that kind of love from her home growing up. Back there, daughters were seen as a burden. Something that needed to be married off as soon as she came of age. Naturally she never had strong feelings for her parents. She didn't even know if they were dead or alive, as long as she was out of that hellhole, she did not care. But she cared a little today and wondered maybe, just maybe what would it be like to grow up in a loving home, to know that your parents were proud of you. Was she jealous of Ahaana now? She hated the idea as much as she hated the woman.

Winning over Vihaan's parents was not going to be a walk in the park. Clearly, they didn't care so much about her as much as they did about their daughter. They didn't even take a second look at her. In a way this worked out perfectly for her because the less obsessed they were about her, the easier it would be to move to America and lesser pressure to come back home. But now that she saw what it was to be loved by parents, to have someone waiting on you anxiously every time you came home, she wanted a little piece of that too. Wasn't she nice to them? She touched their feet to seek their blessings, tried interacting well with Vihaan's mother. But they didn't care. She felt invisible and for the first time she didn't want to be. This strange need rose inside her to become better than Ahaana. To want everything that she had.

It was getting darker outside now and Annie started getting ready to go downstairs to meet the prodigal daughter. She was not even surprised to see Vihaan's parents waiting impatiently in the living room, his father was pacing back and forth in the living room, with occasional glances to the open door. His mother, tidying up the place and rearranging pictures on the coffee table and cushions for the tenth time probably even though none of it needed any rearranging. They were restless and impatient to meet Ahaana. But what was so special about her she thought. Vihaan was there on the couch reading something completely unbothered by the other two. Maybe he really meant it when he said that she was the favorite child.

There was the sound of a car in the distance approaching the farmhouse and they saw the headlights now confirming that someone was coming home.

'I think its her' exclaimed Mr. Khanna looking over at his wife. They both rushed outside and Vihaan too as Annie followed them, the least excited in the group to meet Ahaana.

As Ahaana stepped out into the driveway and made her way towards her parents, there was pin drop silence. Even Annie was curious to see what was going to happen now. She walked up to her parents and looked at them and almost in a whisper and broken voice she said, 'I'.... sorry... Papa.' Mr. Khanna hugged his daughter and cried his heart out and so did Ahaana and her mother. 'We missed you so much.' Said her mother. Ahaana hugged her mom and said, 'I missed you even more. I'm really sorry Mumma.'

'Are you going to do all the meet and greet from here only or do we even get to take her inside?' asked Vihaan.

'Oh yes yes definitely. Come inside.' Said her father.

'You must be hungry no? Look at you. You're so thin! Such a workaholic like your father only I'm sure. Mumma has prepared all your favorite dishes for dinner.' Said her mother holding her face and stroking her hair. As Vihaan walked past his sister carrying her bags, he said in mockery, 'Yeah Mumma's gonna get ya faaat.' She patted him on the shoulder and said, 'Oh, Shut up! I think we all know who used to be the chubby kid here' And they all laughed. Everyone except Annie.

It was a perfect family dinner like the ones Annie had only watched in movies. Parents smothering their daughter with love, they were feeding her more and more even when she told them that she was full. Vihaan being the naughty younger sibling making casual funny remarks at her every now and then but it was evident how sincerely happy he was for her. They had their quirks but they made a great family.

After dinner, they were all sitting in the living room, sharing childhood stories of Ahaana and Vihaan. There was laughter and music and dessert. All of a sudden Vihaan stood up and cleared his throat.

'Okay everyone. I have a small announcement to make.' Everybody was quiet, all eyes were on Vihaan. He continued, 'I gave a lot of thought to how to say this and when and where. But I realized that no other place is going to feel as special as here, where I all my favorite people are. No other time would make me happier than I am right now. So, with all your blessings,' he turned to look at Annie. He walked towards her and went down on one knee. He pulled out a small tiffany box from his pocket. Annie was surprised. She knew he would propose but she really did not think that he would do it in front of his whole family. She would have preferred a more private setting where it would've been just the two of them. But it is happening now and she decided to avoid all the other eyes on her and focus only on Vihaan's handsome face. He continued, a dashing smile playing on his lips and with longing in his eyes, 'Helen, it's been 2 years since we have been in a relationship but when I met you that night, it didn't even take 2 minutes for me know you are the woman I wanted to spend the rest of my life with. Every moment with you felt surreal. You added more meaning to my life and more importantly you are the reason I have all of my favorite people with me in this room right now. If you would let me, I want to spend the rest of my life trying to make you happier than the day before. Will you marry me? Please?'

Helen knew he was a huge romantic at heart but she still wouldn't have expected this. Not in front of his family anyways. Her eyes lit up with happiness and tears and she said, 'Yes'. Even though it started off as her masterplan to get out of the country, she liked him. He was an honest, innocent guy. There was a roar of cheers from Vihaan's parents. They opened a bottle of champagne and started celebrating. But Helen was more curious to know the reaction of only one person. Ahaana was silent and glaring at her now. It felt nice to be under the spotlight for a change, Helen thought. Vihaan's mother was the first one to hug and congratulate her followed by his father and lastly it was Ahaana's turn. She walked towards Helen and hugged her but also whispered something in her ear, 'Looks like you're getting what you wanted.'

'Yeah looks like I am.'

'Well, all the best to you. Sister-in-law.' It didn't take a genius to sense the iciness in Ahaana's voice.

'Thank you,' replied a perplexed Helen.

Chapter - 26

Ahaana

Mr. Khanna was walking back to his room when he saw his daughter pacing nervously in her room. He knocked, 'Hey is everything okay?'

'Yeah, Papa. You haven't slept yet?'

'I was going to but why do I get the feeling that something is bothering you?' he walked towards her and made her sit next to him on the side of her bed.

'Its… its nothing Papa.'

'Listen Pumpkin, this is not my first day as your Papa. I think I know what's bothering you actually.'

'You do?'

'Of course. It's not normal for a daughter to stay away from her family with absolutely no contact for 10 years. But what's even worse is, I failed as a father when I did not even try to reach out to you, even once.'

'Please don't say that Papa. You didn't do anything wrong. Any father would've done the same thing. It was me who acted out of rage and walked out of the house. That was very immature of me.'

'I heard about what happened to him. I'm really sorry about that.' Ahaana was pleasantly surprised to hear her father talk about the one person she never thought she'll discuss with him.

'You might have left us, but I couldn't stop making sure whether you were okay or not. But my pride stopped me from helping you out. I know what you've been through. But I shouldn't have put you through that.' Her father started tearing up and wiped his eyes as he said this.

'But if you think about it, I wouldn't be who I am if I were still under your wing.' She tried cheering him up.

'That's true. So about this girl Helen. Vihaan told us that you've spent time with her before. I don't want to repeat any of my previous mistakes but I am curious to know. What do you think about her?'

Ahaana's facial features became rigid at the mention of her name. Her father was even quicker to notice that. 'It is about her isn't it? One psychiatrist to another, there are certain reflex that we develop over time and certain cues that you don't miss in a person. I know she's hiding something. She's extremely nervous ever since you got here. I thought it was because she was meeting us for the first time. At least that's your Mumma's opinion when I discussed this with her.'

'Papa, we cannot let Vihaan marry her. She's dangerous and he has no idea what he's about to get himself into.'

'What are you talking about?' Mr. Khanna was definitely not expecting that for an answer.

'Papa what I'm about to tell you is very sensitive. That woman cannot be a part of our family. But we have to do this very carefully.'

'Don't worry. As long as I'm alive, I won't let anybody harm my family. You're not alone anymore. Papa is with you. Now tell me who is this woman and what does she want?'

Ahaana woke up to her mom wailing loudly. It must be around 8 in the morning. She ran downstairs chasing the voice of her mother crying. She was joined by her brother also running towards the sound. They reached the front porch of the house to find their dear father sitting lifeless on his chair, newspaper strewn across the floor beside him. They didn't want to believe what they were seeing. Ahaana walked towards her father to check his pulse. With a shocked gasp she let go of his wrist.

'What happened Didi? Please tell me he's fine.'

Ahaana couldn't find any words to convey this news. She only shook her head as her eyes were filled with tears.

The funeral was a small event. To follow up a celebration the previous night with a funeral the very next morning was something none of them saw coming. Ahaana was standing in a corner of the room, too numb to even cry or process this when Annie came and stood behind her. She spoke in a low voice that only Ahaana could hear, 'Aww is little Pumpkin sad that Daddy went away?' Ahaana's eyes opened wide as she heard this remark. She turned around as quickly as she could but there was no one. Did she hallucinate that?

It was late in the evening, all the guests had left and Ahaana was in her mother's room taking care of her. But Ahaana couldn't get her head out of the incident that happened earlier. Hearing Annie's voice and what she said had seriously disturbed Ahaana. It was not the most appropriate time but she needed to get to the depths of this. So, she asked her mother, 'Mumma, what exactly happened in the morning?'

Her mother started sobbing at the mention of her father's death. 'I went to call him for breakfast and that's when I found him lying there....' She started crying again.

'But I remember seeing his coffee on the table and it was only half full.'

'Helen was up early today morning and she made coffee for him today. She told me to sleep in and not worry about it since she was already up. I couldn't even make him one last cup of coffee.'

So what happened earlier that day was not a hallucination. Annie was behind her father's murder. But why? That's when she remembered. Annie called her 'Pumpkin', which was something only her father called her ever since she was a little girl. And yesterday, the only time he called her 'Pumpkin' was when he came into her room and talked about Annie. That could mean only one thing. Annie had overheard their conversation. Annie had killed her father and she was threatening Ahaana to stay away from her and Vihaan. There was only one small problem though. Annie crossed the wrong line this time.

Chapter - 27

Vihaan

Vihaan was on the porch taking a short smoking break after taking care of his father's funeral arrangements. The caterers, florists and event management people had just left and the house went back to a deafening silence. He never thought he'll smoke again and he never felt the need to. But the news of his father passing away hit him hard and there was no other way of coping with this loss. One is never prepared for something like this. He was not the young pampered child of the family anymore. It was up to him now, to take care of his mother and this house and with a heavy heart he realized that it was time to step into his father's shoes. He was distracted when he felt a hand on his shoulder. It was Helen.

'Hey babe, how are you holding up? Wait, are you smoking?'

'Hey, yeah, um... don't worry it's not a habit or anything. I quit smoking a long time ago but ... I don't know, I just needed it today to calm down and think.'

Helen observed him for a moment. She had only seen him as the bright and joyful young man. It was rare if she saw him feeling low or depressed. He was a master multitasker. Never said 'No' to any opportunity. The word 'burn out' didn't even exist in his dictionary and look at him now. He looks like he hasn't showered in well over 24 hours. She could see stubbles of beard on his chin, his hair was disheveled and he was sweaty and a little smelly too.

'Babe look at you! I think maybe you should freshen up. You'll feel better.'

'I just need to be alone now Helen.'

'I'm sorry but you do have that meeting with the American company today and you don't want to look like that.'

Vihaan couldn't believe what she was saying but he told himself to calm down and stay quiet. He looked away not wanting to have this conversation now.

'Why are you not answering me? Are you not planning to do the meeting? We have to close the deal today if we want to get started on the paper works for our visas. Time will fly.'

'WILL YOU JUST SHUT UP??'

Helen did not see that coming.

'Helen! My father just died okay. He DIED! Its not even been a day and you're worried about going to America? Are you like, insane? That deal or America is the last thing on my mind now. I need to be here for my mother and my sister. Forget about me. My sister just met Papa after 10 years and he's gone now. Can you even imagine what she must be feeling?'

'Nobody asked her to leave her family for a boy she just met' muttered Annie under her breath.

'How could you be so insensitive Helen?'

'See there's no point in us arguing about the mistakes your sister made a few years ago. I know this is a difficult time but we do have to think about the future too. Don't we need to start getting things ready to move?'

Vihaan just looked away, avoiding her question. Helen was starting to realize what this meant. 'Wait, don't you want to go to America? Are you seriously thinking of staying here?'

'Would it be so bad? Listen Helen, I just cannot be away from my family now. And it's nice here right? You said you like it here. I can figure out a way to work remotely. Sid can look after the firm for some time and I can still seal the deal with the American company from here.'

'Vihaan, babe, I think you're really tired. Maybe get some rest and we'll talk about it when you're feeling better', Helen's voice was starting to sound desperate, like she was about to lose something precious.

'No this is the time to talk about it. None of what just happened can be reversed. My father is gone and he is not coming back. I've given this a lot of thought and I think this is the best way to do things right now.'

'So, we're never moving to America?'

'Why are you so hung up on that? If I can do the same work from here isn't that actually better?'

'But ... but it's your dream to go live there.'

'No! Not at all. I've already lived there remember? I just thought that with you in my life it would be like a new adventure, starting over at a new place.' He threw the cigarette away, took her hands in his and was looking into her eyes as he spoke now.

'No' Helen pulled her hands away and walked back to the house while still muttering, and her head twitching 'No. This cannot be happening.'

Vihaan was confused now. He never saw her behave this way. Maybe a death of a close one in the family does bring out the worst in everybody.

He stood there for some more time when he got a call. He saw that it was Ahaana.

'Vihaan, we need to go somewhere.'

'Sure, but why are you calling me on my phone when you're inside the house?'

'Because your fiancé cannot know that we are going together. I'll leave first and 10 minutes later you leave the house too. Meet me at the intersection to the highway.'

'What is all this about? Are you still after her?'

'Vihaan I don't have time to explain now. I need you to meet someone. He will tell you everything. Please do this one last thing for me Vihaan. All of us are in danger.'

Vihaan thought about it for a moment. Helen was acting strangely a moment ago, and she was being insensitive too. With the newfound fear for his family's safety now, he decided to agree to his sister's request this time.

'Fine I'll meet you at the intersection in 10.'

Chapter- 28

Alex

It was a pleasant day, actually the perfect day for a vacation. From where he was right now, it almost looked like a vacation too, only if that were true, thought Alex. He made himself a cup of tea using the kettle in his room. He flew in from Jaipur and checked into Hyatt, in Pune early in the morning. He is expecting guests now and the conversation that he is about to have with them is about a very unpleasant chapter in his life. Is he making a mistake by agreeing to this meeting? Maybe there's still time to back out of it. The idea was very tempting. But if he didn't do this now, another young man and his family might pay the price for his silence. Just like what he had endured a long time ago when he married Annie without looking into who she actually was. Those three years took a huge toll on him. Just when he thought he had hit rock bottom, came the divorce to top it all off. But in retrospect, it all worked out well for him eventually.

He went back home to Jaipur with nothing. No wife and no savings in hand. His mother stood by him and told him it was alright, that things will work out for him again because he was a good person. But that was the problem, he always had to be the good person. And being good always got him into trouble. He started a home food business after going back to Jaipur. Very small scale in the beginning. He cooked from home and delivered to nearby places in his father's old Maruti 800. It was getting rusty at his home after his father passed away a long time ago. He rebuilt the car with the help of his friend and started using it to deliver food when orders came from nearby towns and villages. Alex loved to cook, it has always been his passion. Once he started his business, people started loving his food and the demand started growing. He never compromised on the quality and always whipped up something new in the menu. So, there was always something new to look forward to, even for the returning customers. Money started coming in and he hired a few helpers. Soon the demand grew so much that he needed a proper office and an accountant to manage his revenue. He got his company registered and licensed. He started getting catering orders even from far away cities.

One day he got a call from a wealthy Gujarati family in based out of Dubai. Mr. Sanjay Shah, the business tycoon from Gujarat who built his business empire in Dubai and was hosting his only daughter's wedding in Dubai. A lot of VIPs will be attending the wedding and Mr. Shah specifically wanted authentic Gujarati food prepared by Alex but unfortunately at that time Alex did not have enough money, facilities or the manpower to execute something of that scale abroad. He politely declined the offer but Mr. Shah was not ready to take no for an answer. They flew him out to Dubai and told him to only focus on doing what he does best and that they'll take care of the rest. And he did exactly that. His food was a big hit and people were raving about it. Once the wedding was over and as Alex was packing up to leave he went to thank Mr. Shah for giving him such a massive opportunity. That's when Mr. Shah asked Alex why didn't he think about expanding his business. He briefly told him about his journey and how getting divorced led him to start his food business hoping to make a livelihood out of it for himself and his mother. Mr. Shah told Alex that not a lot of people get second chances in life, but if you got one then it was highly likely that you were destined to do something bigger with your life. With Mr. Sanjay's support Alex opened a new office in Dubai and his business started thriving better than ever. Alex and his mother moved to Dubai. 7 years later, he was now the owner of a successful food empire in India and in Dubai.

Life was going smoothly when last week he got a call from Dr. Ahaana Khanna. That one phone call took him back 7 years, right in front of that courthouse where he lost everything and when he was a nobody. He was in Jaipur when Ahaana called him and asked him for more details about Annie. Honestly, Alex wanted to block the call and continue peacefully with his life. That's when she said that her brother was about to get married to her without knowing who she really was. That got Alex's attention. He knew what Annie was capable of but what if Ahaana's brother was too naïve to understand her? And from what she said, it does sound like this guy Vihaan has fallen head over heels for her. But it is not too late now. After thinking about it for a long time Alex agreed to meet Ahaana.

Ahaana came all the way to Jaipur to meet Alex. He was expecting to meet a middle-aged woman based on how matured she sounded on the call. But he was pleasantly surprised to see a beautiful woman. He is someone who travels a lot and have met some of the most beautiful women around the world but she had a charisma that set her apart from all of them. She was so real, even looking stressed and with her panic-stricken eyes, she had an ethereal beauty. They talked in his office. After they talked Ahaana asked if he could talk to her brother directly as he would not listen to her since she did not have any evidence to prove her assumptions. That's when Alex agreed to meet Vihaan in Pune.

As Alex was almost finished with his tea, he heard a doorbell. He opened the door to see the familiar Dr. Ahaana standing in front of him with a young man, who very much resembled her facial features and handsome too behind all that ruggedness. They both looked exhausted and really tired like they've been through something bad. For a moment Alex's brain started thinking of the worst that Annie could do. But if that were the case then they probably wouldn't be standing here in front of him now. Alex welcomed them into his room.

'Hi Doctor' Alex extended a hand to Ahaana.

'Hello Alex,' said Ahaana as she took his hand.

'And you must be Vihaan.' said Alex as he shook his hand.

It was Ahaana's turn to introduce them to each other now, 'Vihaan this is Alex. Helen's ex-husband.'

Vihaan looked at his sister in shock.

Alex said, 'I know this is not a very ideal situation.' But something about their appearance really bothered him. He had to ask, 'Are you guys okay?'

It was Ahaana who spoke now, 'Yeah... our father passed away this morning...'

'Oh, I'm so sorry to hear that. My condolences.'

As he said this he looked at Ahaana and noticed that she had a strange look in her eyes. He could see the fear in them. So, was it not a natural death? Alex did not want to think what his mind was already telling him.

'Please sit guys. Can I get you something?'

'Didi why are we here?' Vihaan's voice had a lot of rage as he hissed the words.

'I think I can maybe explain this better,' said Alex,' I'm sure doctor would have told you what she knew about Annie's life.'

'Her name is Helen' said Vihaan, impatient and the rage even more evident in his voice now.

'No. That woman is Annie. Vihaan, I get that you're angry but don't you think that you need to know who that woman is before you decide to spend the rest of your life with her? And I really couldn't care less whether you marry her or not. Annie is not my problem and that's all I need to know. But your sister here loves you very much and is seriously concerned about your safety and that's the only reason why I'm doing this.'

'I'm sorry. But what is there to even talk about? You abused her. She couldn't tolerate you so she left. I shouldn't even be here.'

'Is that what she told you? I just want to make one thing clear that I never raised my hand on her or any woman.'

'So what about Daisy? How could you keep a child away from her mother? What kind of a monster are you?'

'Vihaan!', said Ahaana in a loud voice to halt him in his insults.

Alex looked at Ahaana and she nodded again. Alex turned to look at Vihaan. He leaned forward in his chair and said with dead seriousness in his eyes 'Vihaan, Annie and I never had a baby. Daisy is only Annie's imagination.'

'What are you saying?' Alex could see the confusion in Vihaan's eyes.

'Please hear me out. When Annie and I began our life in Mumbai, things were really good or at least that's what I thought. But she always wanted the better things in life and that's really fine and I would have given it to her if I could afford any of them. I was just an accountant working at a hospital. I had debts to pay off and our living expenses and she was not ready to share any of the expenses with me. She didn't have a degree so she said she won't get a decent paying job. I was really okay with her working or not. That was her choice after all. When we moved in here, my broker tricked and got me a very shabby apartment. I was disappointed about it too but more importantly I had to make ends meet and I didn't have the time to sit and cry about it. Annie was not happy either and always bugged me about moving to a nicer place. I told her we will do that once we have enough savings. A year went by and one day she asked me if I could help her set up a dance studio for her. I was really glad that finally she found her passion and agreed to help her. But about a week later we found out that we were pregnant. And the worst part is she thinks I did that to her purposely to stop her from working. Why would I bring a child into our lives when the two of us could barely live decently each day? So, I started working overtime for extra money, whatever little I could earn to make my family safe and happy. But that's when I started noticing that Annie was getting a little too obsessed with the baby. Something about her behavior was different. She kept saying that once the baby arrives everything will be okay. She even found a name for her. Daisy. I asked her what if it was a boy but no she was absolutely sure that it will be a girl. It still made me very happy to see how happy she was. Unfortunately, Annie incurred a lot of internal bleeding during labor and... and we lost our baby. And guess what, she was right. It was a baby girl after all.'

Vihaan didn't know what to say now. His anger subsided now replaced with a lot of sympathy for this man and Annie.

'Things took a turn for the worse once we got back to our normal lives again. I thought she could still pursue her idea for a dance studio. But she started acting as if Daisy was still with us. There was a life size baby doll that she had bought for Daisy. She wouldn't keep it down. I was confused at first and when I mentioned this to the doctor he said that some mothers might experience these hallucinations immediately after losing their child. Her hormones were all acting up but she should come to her senses in a few days. It was like Post Traumatic Stress. Weeks passed by and her behavior did not change. One day I decided to clean up the house and move all the toys and baby clothes into these cardboard boxes. Annie was just coming back from church when she saw me tossing that doll into one of the boxes. She just lost it. She came at me like a bull, she yelled at me, slapped me hard and took the doll out of the box, started cooing to her and putting bandages on her. You see, other than these incidents, she was pretty normal for the rest of the time. But I was scared to bring up this in conversation again with her, afraid of another episode.

Home started feeling like a warzone. I didn't know what triggered her anymore. But despite all of this I still loved her so damn much and wanted to help her. Maybe if we had a relative here or a friend that I could talk to, we could get her the help she needed but back then even I wasn't ready to accept that something was going on with her. I started spending more time at work. And sometimes when it rained one of my colleagues, a woman named Rita would drop me home in her car. Her house was a few blocks away from ours. Annie spotted Rita dropping me home a few times and she started making things up in her head. One-night things really got out of hand. It was raining heavily and as usual Rita dropped me home in her car. Once I was inside the apartment, Annie started accusing me of having an affair with Rita. I told her that I wasn't having an affair. She accused me of not spending time with her and Daisy and got really angry and started throwing things at me. I lost my temper in that moment and said that Daisy was not real and that, I think was the tipping point for her. I saw a whole different side of her that night. She started throwing things around violently and pushed me. She was rushing to get out of the apartment with that doll. I couldn't let her go in that condition, so, I went after her. The corridor was very slippery because of the rain. A lot of water had seeped in. I grabbed her hand from the back to stop her from leaving and that's when Annie slipped and fell and hit her head on the floor. She was unconscious for some time. I took her to the nearest clinic I could find. Fortunately, it was nothing serious. But the first thing she asked me when she opened her eyes was 'where is Daisy'. And that's when I knew that I needed to get her help. But I didn't want her to have another violent episode, so, I lied to her and said that Daisy was in the other room and that she was okay. She continued asking me about Daisy for the next few days and one day when I came in to check in on her as usual, she was gone. She was at Mrs. Rodriguez's house and she probably told her the same lie she told your sister. The lady believed her lie, took her in and looked after her. Annie filed for divorce from there and I begged her not to do this. I really wanted to help her get better but she had her mind fixated on divorce. After talking about this to my friend Rahul and in order to get her the treatment she needed, I put that as an unofficial clause in the divorce agreement. I made my lawyer convey to her that I shall willingly sign for the divorce only if she went to the doctor. I thought at least that way she will get the help she needs and maybe she will come to her senses.

My friend Rahul arranged the consultation with Dr. Ahaana. I said I won't talk to the doctor in person so that Annie won't feel like it's a set up but I'll pay for all of her sessions. Few months went by and the divorce came through. I remember she was very happy that day. Later that evening Rahul took me out for a drink but I didn't drink. I told him that I wanted to meet her. He told me to call and talk to her first. I called and it was Mrs. Rodriguez who picked up the call instead of Annie. She was about to hang up on me when I said that Annie was mentally unstable and that we don't have a baby and that she needed to be careful around her. I heard a gasp from Mrs. Rodriguez. Then I heard Annie in the background asking her who is she talking to and I realized that Annie had caught her talking to me. So, I went over to Mrs. Rodriguez's apartment because I had a bad feeling about Annie and no matter how much I pleaded Annie wouldn't let me in. I said I only wanted to talk to her and that if she didn't trust me, then Mrs. Rodriguez could be present there as well. She said immediately that Mrs. Rodriguez was downstairs to collect a courier and that she didn't like having strangers in the house. I knew she was lying because I had just come upstairs and there was nobody down. But it was not just that, from where I was standing, I could see a bedroom and on the floor, I could see an old lady's legs. As if she had fallen down. That's when I knew what was going on and I knew she was beyond help at that point. I didn't know this woman anymore. She's not the Annie I fell in love with when I married her. The truth is, Annie always had these issues since a young age and her parents covered it up and forced her to marry me. But now she had become a killer. The craziest part is how smoothly she lied to me about it with a straight face. It really doesn't affect her. She would kill anyone in a heartbeat.'

Ahaana continued now, 'When I went to Mrs. Rodriguez's apartment a month later the neighbors said that according to Annie, the night when Mrs. Rodriguez died, she had an early supper and went to bed around 9:30 PM. Alex talked to the same woman at 11:00 PM on the same night and Rahul also verified this. I know it's a lot but please you need to understand that she is a murderer and she did not stop with Mrs. Rodriguez.' Ahaana's voice was broken now.

'What do you mean?' asked Vihaan still trying to process all this new information about his fiancé.

'Last night, Papa and I were talking in my room. I told him everything I knew about her and about my meeting with Alex. I said that we needed to stop this wedding. It was Papa's idea to ask Alex to come down here and talk to you. But she found out. Today morning she killed Papa by poisoning his morning coffee.'

'How can you be sure that she did that?'

'Mumma said that Helen was up early today and insisted on making coffee for Papa.'

Alex was shocked at this news too. She has unleashed that demon again. He blamed himself for Ahaana and Vihaan losing their dear father. Only if he had given her the help she needed back then, he could have spared one more life.

'Guys, not to freak you out but where is Annie right now?' asked Alex suddenly realizing that they have one more parent left back home.

Vihaan was the one to answer, 'She's back at the farmhouse with Mumma. Wait, oh my god! We left our mother with a killer in the house.'

'But she doesn't know that you're with me, right?' asked Ahaana.

'I'm really sorry about this, but we were already fighting and I didn't want to upset her even more. So, when she asked me where I was going, I told her that I was going out with you.'

'Oh my god! Vihaan. Come on, we need to get home as soon as possible.' Said Ahaana as she dashed towards the door.

Chapter - 29

It was almost midnight now. There were a couple of police cars in the compound of the farmhouse. Mrs. Khanna and Vihaan were severely wounded in the head and were being given medical attention in the ambulance. The police had questioned the mother and the son and were speaking to Ahaana now.

The officer was a middle-aged man who looked absolutely irritated that he was dragged into this mess so late at night. Judging by his pot belly, sulky attitude, and terrible mood, Ahaana could tell that he couldn't wait to wrap this up and go home.

'So tell me once again, you and your brother came home and you were attacked?' asked the officer.

'No, Sir. We got home and saw our mother lying unconscious on the floor, she was bleeding and it looked like a fresh wound, so, I knew the attack happened right before we reached here. We split up to look for her and my brother got hit next. He probably called for you before losing consciousness. I ran towards the sound of him screaming but she was hiding behind a door and hit me and I can't remember anything after that.' repeated Ahaana impatiently for the third time now.

'Right. And you think you lost any valuables doctor?'

'I don't think so.'

'What do you think was the motive?'

'I don't know Sir. She used to be my patient before. A very long time ago. But then she stopped coming to see me and left the city altogether. Naturally, I was against my brother marrying her and she hated me when I tried to talk him out of it. Once she is obsessed with something, either she needs to have it or no one else should have it. That's just how she feels in her head.'

'Okay, do one thing. Write down a complaint at the station and we'll look for her.'

Ahaana looked at Vihaan and then turned to look back at the officer. 'We don't have any complaint Sir.'

'Huh?! You were just attacked.'

'Yes, but we didn't lose anything.'

'What if she comes back again?'

'Sir she needs medical attention right now not police and court. It will only make things worse. But if we ever feel threatened by her again, then we'll definitely file a complaint Sir. Can we do that?'

The officer had a confused look on his face. He took one long good look at each one of them and said, 'Fine. Who cares? If you don't have a complaint then why should I even bother? Come on guys, we're done here.' He called out to the other officers.

The police and the medical staff left after a few minutes. Once they were alone, Vihaan asked his sister, 'Why did you tell them that we did not have any complaint?'

Ahaana turned to look at him and said, 'You would rather I file a complaint and spend the rest of our lives trying to hunt her down? Are you new to the legal system here? You think you can spend the next few decades of your life going in and out of court until they get fed up and write this off? Vihaan my intention was to never harm her. I only wanted to get her the help she needed. And so, did Papa too.'

'But what if she comes back? She's a killer on the loose.'

'Vihaan if there's something I know about her, she's always looking for an escape. Her escape from her past life from Alex and Mrs. Rodrigues was you. Once she's hurt someone, she'll avoid them and even that city at any cost. She was only with you because she wanted to go and settle in America and get far away from all this. And once you made it clear to her that it was not happening, that was her trigger to attack us. She's probably moved on to her next escape plan, whatever or whoever it is. And don't worry. As long as I'm here I won't let anything bad happen to our family. You have my word.' Ahaana held Vihaan's face as she made that promise. Vihaan hugged his sister. He was crying now, blaming himself for all the time when he didn't listen to her. Maybe if he had, his father would still be here today. 'I'm really sorry Didi!'

Ahaana hugged him tightly and patted his hair and said, 'Don't worry, it's all over now.'

Chapter - 30

2 years later...

It was a Friday and Ahaana was done with her last client for the day. She heard a knock at the door and it was her assistant. She peeked in through the door and asked, 'That was your last consultation for the day Doctor. Is there anything else you'd like me to reschedule apart from blocking out the weekend and any other engagements until Tuesday?'

Ahaana thought for a second and replied, 'No Nancy, that should be all. In fact, why don't you take off early?'

'Oh, its alright Doctor. I can stay.'

'No. It's the weekend. Go out, have fun! You don't want to end up as a workaholic like me. Go on. I'll see you on Tuesday.'

'Thank you Doctor. Have a good weekend.'

'Will do!'

Ahaana waited until she heard the door close to make sure that Nancy took off. Perfect! She made herself a cup of steaming hot green tea and kicked off her heels and slid down on the couch in her office. On those rare days when she was done with work early, she liked to chill for a little bit at her office and get comfortable before going home. It must have been a few minutes when her phone rang on the table. Vihaan's name flashed on the screen. Excitedly Ahaana jumped up and walked to her office table to pick it up.

Vihaan was practically almost yelling on the other side, there was a lot of pounding music in the background. 'Didi, what time are you getting here?'

'About 12 at night. Hey don't worry about it, besides from the sound of that party I doubt that you'll be sober by then. I'll get a cab.'

'No no the boys insisted but I'm not drinking. You know that I didn't want this. Besides who celebrates a bachelor party before an engagement? They are idiots.'

Ahaana laughed, 'Hey loosen up a little dude. You don't have to be so perfect all the time. This weekend is all about fun.'

'Yeah I'll have fun after you get home safely.'

'Fine. I'll try to get in early so that you can have fun. I'll see you soon.'

'Okay let me know when you board the flight. Alright?'

'Yes Sir!'

Ahaana was so happy for Vihaan. He was getting engaged to Mehr on Sunday. They really did make a beautiful couple. But more importantly, Mehr was the right choice for Vihaan. She was a couple of years younger than him and they practically grew up together because her father was a cardiologist and in the same social circle as their father. She was beautiful, educated and a lovely girl who had a small pastry business which she built herself. She was a perfect fit for their family. Yeah this is nice she thought. This is how it's supposed to be.

She put the phone down on the table. It was a nice mahogany table she thought as she walked around the edge of the table, tracing a finger over it. The table was from the 1800s and she had bought it from an antique store. The thing with ancient things was that they came with some secrets. She too had a little secret of her own. Her lips twitched into a strange smile. She was sitting at her chair now and right underneath the table there were two small bolts, hidden to anyone who looked at the table normally. You could only unlock it from the bottom. She unlocked the bolts and opened the top part of the table to reveal a small chamber inside. She picked out a wedding ring with a bunch of hair tucked into it, everything secured tight with a red ribbon. It was the same ring that Vihaan gave to Annie when he had proposed to her that night at the farmhouse and the hair on the ring belonged to Annie!

After Ahaana and Vihaan left Alex's hotel room and rushed back to their farmhouse, they knew something had gone terribly wrong. The house was very quiet, there was absolute pin drop silence and the lights were off. They walked inside to find their mother bleeding in the living room. Both of them rushed towards her. They tried waking her up and Vihaan took his phone out and called the police. They lifted her slowly and placed her onto the couch and were still in shock when the second blow came from behind. This time hitting Vihaan. Vihaan cried out in pain at the unexpected attack. Ahaana let out a scream but her hands were faster. She blocked the hit that was coming for her next. And that's when she saw Annie, looking like a deranged lunatic on the loose. She looked like she had lost sense of her reality and had transformed into someone else. There was a metal rod in her hand covered in blood. Ahaana pushed her away with every ounce of force she could muster from her body. But Annie came and took another swing at Ahaana, who was quick to dodge that as well. Ahaana kicked Annie in her stomach and that's when Annie's head hit a wall and lost her consciousness.

When Annie opened her eyes again, she was in an underground cellar. It was dark and dimly lit. As she looked around the place she was jump scared by someone sitting in front of her. It was Ahaana and it looked like she had a wound on the side of her head which was stitched up now. But Annie did not remember hitting her.

'Oh, Madam is awake!' said Ahaana in mock exclamation.

'Where am I?' asked Annie in a groggy voice. She was tied into a wooden chair her hands and feet chained tightly to it.

'Here drink some water. We need to have a little chat.' Ahaana opened a bottle and poured some water into Annie's mouth. Since Annie was gagged for a long time, and her throat felt dry, she gulped down as much water as she could.

'This is our underground wine cellar next to the house. It was built during the British rule and we thought a lot about changing up this space, but it was too good to break apart. You know, they build things to last. This place for example is sound proofed very well. Even if you scream at the top of your lungs no one is going to hear you' said Ahaana.

Annie looked around at the old cellar. It looked more like a dungeon or a torture chamber. 'What happened to your head?' asked Annie.

'Oh this. Yeah, things I do for you. You see I had to make it look convincing enough in front of the cops. So, after I got you down here while my mother and Vihaan were passed out, I had to improvise and hit myself with that rod to make it look like you attacked me and got away. Don't worry the police won't be coming after you. I took care of that.' Ahaana smiled wildly at Annie. She probably wished that the she was in police custody now.

'Now tell me what did you do to my father?' Ahaana's smile faded and she was dead serious now, her eyes shooting daggers at Annie.

Annie smirked, 'You wouldn't leave me alone. I mean I tried warning you but you won't listen. Killing you would be way too easy. I wanted you to suffer. Knowing everything but being unable to do anything about it. But why did you have to go and complain to your Papa?' asked Annie imitating a childlike voice, 'So, I had to take somebody out of the equation.'

'Just like you took Mrs. Rodriguez out of the equation?'

Annie's eyes shot up at Ahaana. She smiled at her, 'You know, you really are smart. Then why do you go around doing dumb things like digging into my past? See with Mrs. Rodriguez I had no intention to kill her. Not initially at least.' Annie paused to cough, 'She really was very sweet. When the divorce came through and I told her that I'll move out of her place she insisted that I stay there and that I'll never have to worry about money because apparently, she had added my name in her will. That woman was loaded you know?' she stopped, coughing a little more and continued, 'Only if my idiot ex-husband hadn't called her that night and told her that I was crazy, I wouldn't have hurt her. I could see her expression change the second she knew that the problem was me and not him. Ah poor Alex. He's always been like that. But now I had to take care of her, didn't I? She knew too much. I added a little extra painkillers into her nighttime chamomile tea. I wanted to give her a painless death after all.' The coughing has increased now.

Ahaana was watching her intently now. She asked, 'What did you do to my Papa Annie?' Annie looked down smiling and then looked up at her, 'You know they say that you shouldn't repeat the same method just because it was successful once. Well look who is laughing now! All I did was try to give a pain free death to your father too. Vihaan would ultimately only do what his Papa wanted him to do. So, between you and your father, I thought it made more sense that he went down first. That way I could watch you suffer.' she started coughing more. 'But I didn't think that Vihaan would put off our plan to move to America just because the old man died. That's where I made a mistake. I didn't see that coming. I really should've taken you out. And with America out of the picture, what was even the point of marrying that fool? To spend the rest of my life here? Constantly running from the police for the rest of my life?'

'So, you decided to kill all of us and make your grand escape. Well played Annie! Talking about grand escapes, how are you feeling now?'

She started coughing more and splattered some blood onto her dress this time. There was a familiar tension on her face, 'What is happening to me? Did you inject something into me, you bitch?' Annie was breathing faster, gasping for air now.

'No no no what would be the fun in that? I agree with you, revenge is only fun when you get to watch them suffer. How was that water you had earlier? Tasty? All it took was a little bit of fish oil mixed into it to trigger your allergy. It should have fully entered your bloodstream now. I would say you have a few minutes at the most.' said Ahaana in a deadbeat tone, each word piercing Annie's ears while a chill just ran down her spine. Ahaana sat back in her chair watching Annie wriggle in her chair gasping for breath and thoroughly enjoying it. 'No…help… me…..' Annie was trying hard to speak now but barely any words came out of her.

'You know Annie, I'll tolerate anything but you played dirty when you messed with my family.' Annie watched and she saw a darkness in Ahaana's eyes. The eyes of a predator enjoying its prey suffer in pain. 'I met my Papa after 10 long years and you had to take him away from me. Do you even know how that feels?'

Annie couldn't even utter a word now. She was struggling harder to breath with every passing second, her chest heaving up and down harder and she was gasping for more air. Her face was turning purple now, eyes popping out and green veins were starting to protrude on her skin. She started making noises, like somebody was twisting her windpipes.

'It's time for your grand escape Annie. And this is Goodbye forever.'

She made a loud gasping sound as she attempted to breathe one last time, with the last bit of energy left in her body and she stopped moving. Her body was bloated and cold now. Ahaana moved Annie into their fruit orchard. They had a huge furnace near the orchard to burn all the farm waste on the compound. It was loaded already and Ahaana threw Annie's body into the furnace and lit the fire. By the next morning, there won't be any trace of Annie. But before she burned Annie, she had taken her engagement ring and cut off a thick chunk of her hair. She loved collecting souvenirs after all.

She reached into the chamber in the table to take out two more things from inside. A dog collar with the name tag 'Johnny' and a small chunk of half burnt sports shoes with the letters 'Jay' engraved on it.

Vihaan was only a five-year-old little boy when he came home crying that evening with a bite mark on his leg. The neighbor's dog Johnny chased him through the ground and attacked him. Nobody could hurt her little brother. If her neighbors couldn't control their dog then she will do whatever it takes to protect her brother.

And that boy Jay who was the captain of the school football team, teased Vihaan in front of the other kids and wouldn't let him play football. He said that Vihaan was short and fat. That was rude! Vihaan cried a lot that night while a storm was brewing inside her. Her parents ignored all of this obviously because they didn't even know how much Vihaan loved playing football. And if Jay had a problem with her brother playing, well then, he should be out of the team. Football after all is a game only played by those with strong legs. What would he do if he lost his prized legs? At that year's Holi celebration, he got the answer for that. The boy spent the next few years on a wheelchair due to nerve damage on his legs, while Vihaan was selected into the school's football team. She still remembers how happy he was that day!

As she placed her souvenirs back inside the chamber, another thought struck her.

How much did she actually know about this girl Mehr?

What if she hurt Vihaan?

The End

www.ingramcontent.com/pod-product-compliance
Lightning Source LLC
LaVergne TN
LVHW041929070526
838199LV00051BA/2755